Hans Christian Andersen's
Fairy Tales

Hans Christian Andersen's
FAIRY TALES
ILLUSTRATED BY
KAY NIELSEN

FOREWORD BY JOAN D. VINGE,
HUGO AWARD-WINNING AUTHOR OF *THE SNOW QUEEN*

RACEHORSE PUBLISHING

First published in 1924 by George H. Doran Company

First Racehorse Publishing Edition 2017
Foreword © 2017 Joan D. Vinge

Racehorse Publishing books may be purchased in bulk at special discounts for sales promotion, corporate gifts, fund-raising, or educational purposes. Special editions can also be created to specifications. For details, contact the Special Sales Department, Skyhorse Publishing, 307 West 36th Street, 11th Floor, New York, NY 10018 or info@skyhorsepublishing.com.

Racehorse Publishing™ is a pending trademark of Skyhorse Publishing, Inc.®, a Delaware corporation.

Visit our website at www.skyhorsepublishing.com.

10 9 8 7 6 5 4 3 2 1

Library of Congress Cataloging-in-Publication Data is available on file.

Print ISBN: 978-1-63158-133-5
Ebook ISBN: 978-1-63158-134-2

Cover and interior artwork by Kay Nielsen

Printed in China

Contents

In the night the dog came again, took the princess on his back and ran with her to the soldier.

[See Page 9]

Illustrations

Illustrations—*continued*

FOREWORD

Once upon a time, in the late 1970s, I wrote a novel called *The Snow Queen*. It was one of many retellings of the classic Hans Christian Andersen fairy tale that is included in this book. Inspired by a story that was approximately 12,600 words long (his longest fairy tale), I wrote a novel that was almost five hundred pages long.

Could there really be so much left unsaid in "The Snow Queen" that I'd needed five hundred pages to fill it out? No, though like most fairy tales, even Andersen's longest stories are stripped to basics.

Philip Pullman, author of the classic fantasy trilogy His Dark Materials, has said that his lifelong love of fairy tales came from their "wonderful shallowness. They have no depth, no psychology," he wrote in a 2013 essay. "The [characters] don't fret about their feelings; they often don't appear to know that they have any feelings. Everything they do is on the surface, because the surface is all there is."

And yet he also said, "Fairy stories loosen the chains of the imagination. They give you things to think with—images to think with—and the sense that all kinds of things are possible."

Controversial opinions, especially from a writer, and yet they hold truth: Fairy tale collections are full of stories that seem to have been made up by children; they are so short and lacking in detail. But their cores have risen out of the deep subconscious of humanity, so they resonate in the minds of people who encounter them and their intangible magic makes them unforgettable.

In the millennia before the distractions of modern entertainment, or even literacy, telling a good story (sometimes putting it to a tune; folk ballads have a similar history) could provide relief from a day's grueling work or the boredom of long winter evenings. The need to cobble together incidents made up on the spur of the moment might cause holes in the plot; incidents and themes might repeat from one tale to another, causing the kind of "wonderful shallowness" Philip Pullman referred to. Also, because these were stories for people living in a harsh world, harsh things befell some characters . . . and those characters who survived, good or evil, tended to simply go on their way, unmoved.

There were no books in which to record the earliest stories, but a popular tale would remain in the minds of tellers and listeners, and be shared with others. Their "best parts" would be embellished and their plot holes filled in, but other details would be forgotten. As a result, the most popular stories would spread to new audiences and continue to be told down through time, but names and details would morph as society itself changed until eventually, with the development of writing, they became written tales . . . although that didn't stop their magical transformations.

Possibly the oldest folktale of all involves an enchanted stone, or something like it: the One Ring of Power forged from mithril, King Arthur's sword trapped in an enchanted rock, David's slingstone in the Bible . . . and older still, there is an ancestor to these stories dating back tens of thousands of years among the Aborigines of Australia. They still tell the tale of a stone with god-like powers that helped save the people "from the ice," probably during the last Ice Age.

Considering that indigenous Australians were separated from Europeans and European lore for at least fifty thousand years, this tale has existed for an unbelievable amount of time—possibly beginning with a common source that spread by telling the story over and over through time . . . or perhaps independently, because the same "magical" source of storytelling could exist in every human brain.

Once stories started to be written down, two types of folk tradition began to coexist: the original oral tradition and the "literary" one, in which tales recorded by collectors were influenced by whoever wrote them down. The writer tended to improve the plot, smooth out the narrative, and mix in his or her own ideas and character motivations.

"Fairy tales," or written folktales as we know them now, did not gain an official name until the mid-seventeenth century, with the publication in France of the first stories called "contes des fées," or "fairy tales" (given the name by writer Marie-Catherine d'Aulnoy because most of the tales included fairies, elves, and other supernatural creatures). Fairy tales became a fad, *en vogue* in intellectual circles during the reign of Louis XIV. Charles Perrault, the best remembered of the fairy tale writers, recorded a number of folktales that are still famous including "Cinderella" and "Little Red Riding Hood."

Eventually the fad passed and fairy tales became passé for over a century. Then, in the early 1800s—a time when the French occupied Germany—German folklorists Jacob and Wilhelm Grimm once again began collecting folk stories, determined to record as much of Germany's traditional lore as possible before it was lost. They gathered stories from many sources—including educated friends who'd heard the tales from their nannies and grandmothers—as well as from the *volk*, or "common people."

As a result, the brothers wound up quietly revising the "genuine" tales in the first published edition of their collection *Children's and Household Tales* (published in 1812 and known in English as *Grimms' Fairy Tales*). They altered them to sound more "rustic," as well as toned down the graphic details that would have offended middle-class readers in the mid-nineteenth century. Over the years they continued to add more tales to newer editions of the book, and also further reduced the darkest and most violent content. As a result, the book is still in print and their most popular stories are familiar to people around the world, like the works of Perrault.

But the most memorable stories in the collection you are about to read, by the Danish author Hans Christian Andersen, are equally as popular and unforgettable in a way that makes them unique, just as Andersen himself was.

He was born in 1805, the son of a shoemaker. Orphaned when he was quite young, he lived a difficult life until he was adopted by a patron who saw the promise of his talent and imagination.

He had probably heard Danish fairy tales from his mother and grandmother as a child, and reading no doubt exposed him to others because the Grimm brothers' collection first came out when he was eight years old. In any case, he seems to have absorbed the subliminal language of folktales, filled with symbolism from earlier times, which inevitably found its way into his own work.

He became a prolific writer of plays, travelogues, novels, and poems as well, but is best remembered for his fairy tales.

He was a devout Christian and unlike the Grimms or Perrault, he does not seem to have struggled to insert Christian references into tales that were remnants of traditions dating back to the Bronze Age or earlier.

In fact, in many of his stories he seems to have had to struggle to find a way to insert magical beings. Tales like "The Steadfast Tin Soldier" or "The Snow Queen," even though they had fantastic elements, did not really require the presence of evil gnomes or wicked witches. Also, his stories tended to be less graphically violent than the folktales passed down uncensored from a time when he would have found them not just unthinkable, but unbearable. However, what makes them hard to forget is that they are often wrenchingly sad.

Andersen was a tall, gangly man with a large nose, a personality that nowadays might be called "geek-like," and the sensitivity of an artist. His past had left him insecure and lonely; he fell in love easily and took the inevitable rejections of his proposals hard. As a result, he often felt profoundly depressed. His past may have had a lot to do with the fact that his fairy tales were unlike others, in that they emphasized emotional pain rather than the physical suffering in the "flat superficial stories with emotionless characters" that Philip Pullman described. Furthermore, Andersen's "good" characters not only suffer, they often don't get the happy ending they deserve—like real people and like Andersen himself. Equally ironic, the villains seem to vanish unpunished.

Andersen created most of his stories from his own imagination and instilled them with deeply religious, middle-class morals. However, there is no question that they are "fairy tales," in which he also made use of familiar tropes from much older works. "The Snow Queen," for example, echoes other fairy tales in its story about a young woman seeking her lost love—its antecedents include the northern European "East of the Sun and West of the Moon" and "Eros and Psyche," a classical Greek myth, even though all three vary considerably from one another in their details.

Andersen's best-known fairy tales remain today as widely popular as ever, like the tales of Perrault and the Grimms. Just as they had been retold dozens of times before the emergence of the versions we think of as "original," they have been retold dozens of times since, in one variation or another, nowadays most often as illustrated books or animated films for children.

Of all the tales I was exposed to, Andersen's resonated with me on the deepest level. But more often than not, the unhappy endings had the most powerful emotional effect. For years, stories like "The Little Mermaid" and "The Steadfast Tin Soldier" remained in my mind like sand in my shoes. I actually longed for "Disney versions" of them because I felt sure Disney Studios would give the stories happier endings, which they did, even though that meant "Prince" (my nickname for the stereotypical male hero) had to come to the rescue in "The Little Mermaid" (even though she saved him first). As for the brave, loyal one-legged soldier and his beloved ballerina, they were happily reunited in a five-minute segment of Disney's *Fantasia 2000*, instead of being burned up in the stove together for no reason after his long struggle to get home to her.

But not all of Andersen's original tales resulted in unhappy endings. "The Tinderbox" ended happily in Andersen's version—if you don't mind the soldier killing the witch and stealing the tinderbox just because he was curious about it, or that when his three giant magic dogs came to his rescue at the end, they massacred the townsfolk and killed the king and queen. The princess married the soldier anyway (since her parents had kept her locked in a copper castle and never let her out) and the couple ruled happily ever after. But there was a flatness to the tale, for all that, because, as in so many traditional folk stories, all the characters were ciphers.

Unlike Philip Pullman, I want characters who have genuine emotions tied to what they do, which lends far deeper meaning to a story. I don't find that the added depth detracts from my ability to enjoy the magic, but rather enhances it.

Many writers have felt, as I have, that they'd like to try casting their own magic cloak over the bare bones of a fairy story. After years of wishing I could change a story that I could neither forget nor ever enjoy into something more satisfying, I finally became a writer—able to make my own wishes come true.

Much to my surprise, the first story I actually published was called "Tin Soldier," inspired by Hans Christian Andersen's own "Steadfast Tin Soldier." My retelling was a science fiction novella and my tin soldier was a war veteran with artificial body parts. His ballerina was a female spacer who wrote poetry. I arranged a "happily ever after" for them . . . albeit a bittersweet one because, much as I like a happy ending, I knew that "a fairy tale ending" now means "unrealistically happy" and if I wanted modern readers to resonate with my version, I needed to acknowledge that it wasn't a fairy tale.

As a teenager, I had my first encounter with my other favorite Andersen fairy tale, "The Snow Queen," in the form of a Russian animated film. I was at that awkward age where I thought animation was childish. I didn't see the movie again until I was in my twenties. By then, in the late seventies, I had studied anthropology in college and was using it to "build worlds" in my science fiction writing. I was also married to someone who had taught me to appreciate animation, and we watched the animated "Snow Queen" on television. This time it was pure serendipity.

I was in the process of developing my next novel, and I was pondering a plot where a young woman goes in search of her missing lover. The seventies were a time when more women were writing science fiction, a reverberation of the feminist movement in the late sixties where strong female protagonists were still few and far between in the genre. I wanted to tell a story where "Prince" didn't claim all the heroic action, a story with a woman as the hero, and as many other women as possible playing different roles, both supporting and standing against her.

At the time I had been reading Robert Graves's book *The White Goddess*, a detailed exploration of the ancient religions of Europe and the evidence that they centered on a Creator Goddess. It was very dense with detail, but still so fascinating that I didn't want to stop reading. I'd also found an article linking ancient myths to folktales through recurring symbolic motifs. For example, the striking description of the princess in "Snow White," whose "skin as white as snow, hair as black as ebony (or sometimes night) and lips as red as roses (or sometimes blood)" gives her the three colors of the Goddess, who is often referred to as having a triple aspect portrayed with three faces—the Maiden, the Mother, and the Crone—symbolizing youth, maturity, and old age (also rebirth) in people, and the world itself as it passes through the seasons. Each of them is associated with a color—white, red, and black.

As ancient belief systems were replaced by newer ones, their traditions gradually degenerated into fragments of stories everyone knew, but didn't remember the meaning of—as only the symbols remained, without meaning, in

"Snow White." The three aspects of the Goddess have become separate people: Snow White, the king's daughter; her stepmother; and a crone—the stepmother after she had used magic to transform herself, in order to fool Snow White.

In the end, Snow White is saved by a Prince, of course, because the new world religious order had become far more patriarchal. The huntsman and the seven dwarfs were also portrayed as good, kindly male characters. As usual in fairy tales, the heroine was a helpless young woman, while other female characters, the queen and the crone—the ones who had power—were invariably evil.

Having that archetypal pattern, and my desire to turn it upside down, in mind while watching *The Snow Queen*, I began to realize that this fairy tale was different. *There was no Prince.* Kai, the little boy, was the helpless victim who was enchanted and carried off by the Snow Queen, an elemental spirit of winter. The villain was not just another evil woman . . . she was a goddess.

But in true fairy tale fashion, the fearless, terribly overmatched hero(ine)—little Gerda, Kai's best friend—sets out to find him. The first thing she does is climb into a boat and offers the river her best shoes, asking it to take her to Kai. Making an offering to a body of water goes back to a time when people believed that the river's spirit would grant their wish in return. The Romans did it; even today we toss a coin into a fountain or well and make a wish, even though we no longer have any idea why.

The journey begins, and Gerda faces a series of adventures as she looks for Kai, and every human with any power that she encounters is female. The only male characters are talking animals—a crow and a stag, animals associated with the aspects of the Goddess. Gerda travels north until she comes to the land where winter always dwells (a metaphor for death), and there she finds the Snow Queen's palace and Kai sitting alone inside with only pieces of ice for toys. The Snow Queen is not even there.

Gerda's warmth and tears melt Kai's frozen soul, and he recognizes her. They make the long journey home. However, in Andersen's tale (though not the film), by the time they finally arrive home they have oddly become young adults. But Gerda's grandmother, who told them stories, is there waiting for them and reads them a Bible passage about "having the innocent hearts of children," which seems to ease their minds.

Although its ending is rather anticlimactic (we never even see the Snow

Queen again), and the Bible passage apparently causing everyone's thoughts to backpedal from a potential marriage proposal is awkward, "The Snow Queen" inspired my imagination on another level entirely. It is a story seemingly drawn from traditions that existed long before the overlay of "Prince" came to dominate folktales like this—a story which focused on female characters.

I realized Andersen's fairy tale had given me the golden thread to spin and weave into the story I wanted to write, and showed that a cast of female characters could work very well. (I made the talking animals into significant male human characters in the novel because its universe was not "for womenonly," any more than for men only. To me, a feminist has always been first and foremost a humanist.)

I have always wondered why Andersen chose to write what, in his time, was such a widdershins take on a fairy tale. He wrote other stories with female protagonists, but they weren't endowed with the same determination to seek out the lover they'd lost no matter what like Gerda was.

In any case, her story allowed me to create the book I had been seeking inspiration for. Hans Christian Andersen has my heartfelt gratitude for telling Gerda's story, along with so many other tales that have stayed in people's memories and imaginations ever since.

—Joan D. Vinge

THE · TINDER · BOX

THE TINDER BOX

HERE came a soldier marching along the high road—*one, two! one, two!* He had his knapsack on his back and a sabre by his side, for he had been in the wars, and now he wanted to go home. And on the way he met with an old witch: she was very hideous, and her under lip hung down upon her breast. She said, "Good evening, soldier. What a fine sword you have, and what a big knapsack! You're a proper soldier! Now you shall have as much money as you like to have."

"I thank you, you old witch!" said the soldier.

"Do you see that great tree?" quoth the witch; and she pointed to a tree which stood beside them. "It's quite hollow inside. You must climb to the top, and then you'll see a hole, through which you can let yourself down and get deep into the tree. I'll tie a rope round your body, so that I can pull you up again when you call me."

"What am I to do down in the tree?" asked the soldier.

"Get money," replied the witch. "Listen to me. When you come down to the earth under the tree, you will find your-

1

self in a great hall: it is quite light, for many hundred lamps are burning there. Then you will see three doors; these you can open, for the keys are in the locks. If you go into the first chamber, you'll see a great chest in the middle of the floor; on this chest sits a dog, and he's got a pair of eyes as big as two teacups. But you need not care for that. I'll give you my blue-checked apron, and you can spread it out upon the floor; then go up quickly and take the dog, and set him on my apron; then open the chest, and take as many farthings as you like. They are of copper: if you prefer silver, you must go into the second chamber. But there sits a dog with a pair of eyes as big as mill wheels. But do not you care for that. Set him upon my apron, and take some of the money. And if you want gold, you can have that, too—in fact, as much as you can carry—if you go into the third chamber. But the dog that sits on the money-chest there has two eyes as big as the round tower of Copenhagen. He is a fierce dog, you may be sure, but you needn't be afraid, for all that. Only set him on my apron, and he won't hurt you; and take out of the chest as much gold as you like."

"That's not so bad," said the soldier. "But what am I to give you, you old witch? for you will not do it for nothing, I fancy."

"No," replied the witch, "not a single farthing will I have. You shall only bring me an old tinder box which my grandmother forgot when she was down there last."

"Then tie the rope round my body," cried the soldier.

"Here it is," said the witch, "and here's my blue-checked apron."

Then the soldier climbed up into the tree, let himself slip down into the hole, and stood, as the witch had said, in the great hall where the many hundred lamps were burning.

Now he opened the first door. Ugh! there sat the dog with eyes as big as teacups, staring at him. "You're a nice fellow!" exclaimed the soldier; and he set him on the witch's apron, and took as many copper farthings as his pockets would hold, and then locked the chest, set the dog on it again, and went into the second chamber. Aha! there sat the dog with eyes as big as mill wheels.

"You should not stare so hard at me," said the soldier; "you might strain your eyes." And he set the dog upon the witch's apron. When he saw the silver money in the chest, he threw away all the copper money he had, and filled his pockets and his knapsack with silver only. Then he went into the third chamber. Oh, but that was horrid! The dog there really had eyes as big as the round tower, and they turned round and round in his head like wheels.

"Good evening," said the soldier; and he touched his cap, for he had never seen such a dog as that before. When he had looked at him a little more closely, he thought, "That will do," and lifted him down to the floor, and opened the chest. Mercy! what a quantity of gold was there! He could buy with it the whole of Copenhagen, and the sugar-pigs of the cake-woman, and all the tin soldiers, whips, and rocking-horses in the whole world. Yes, that was a quantity of money! Now the soldier threw away all the silver coin with which he had filled his pockets and his knapsack, and took gold instead: yes, all his pockets, his knapsack, his boots, and his cap were filled, so that he could scarcely walk. Now, indeed, he had plenty of money. He put the dog on the chest, shut the door, and then called up through the tree, "Now pull me up, you old witch."

"Have you the tinder box?" asked the witch.

"Plague on it!" exclaimed the soldier, "I had clean forgotten that." And he went and brought it.

The witch drew him up, and he stood on the high road again, with pockets, boots, knapsack, and cap full of gold.

"What are you going to do with the tinder box?" asked the soldier.

"That's nothing to you," retorted the witch. "You've had your money—just give me the tinder box."

"Nonsense!" said the soldier. "Tell me directly what you're going to do with it, or I'll draw my sword and cut off your head."

"No!" cried the witch.

So the soldier cut off her head. There she lay! But he tied up all his money in her apron, took it on his back like a bundle, put the tinder box in his pocket, and went straight off towards the town.

4

That was a splendid town! He put up at the very best inn, asked for the finest rooms, and ordered his favourite dishes, for now he was rich, having got so much money. The servant who had to clean his boots certainly thought them a remarkably old pair for such a rich gentleman; but he had not bought any new ones yet. The next day he procured proper boots and handsome clothes. Now our soldier had become a fine gentleman; and the people told him of all the splendid things which were in their city, and about the king, and what a pretty princess the king's daughter was.

"Where can one get to see her?" asked the soldier.

"She is not to be seen at all," said they all together; "she lives in a great copper castle, with a great many walls and towers round about it; no one but the king may go in and out there, for it has been prophesied that she shall marry a common soldier, and the king can't bear that."

"I should like to see her," thought the soldier; but he could not get leave to do so. Now he lived merrily, went to the theatre, drove in the king's garden, and gave much money to the poor; and this was very kind of him, for he knew from old times how hard it is when one has not a shilling. Now he was rich, had fine clothes, and gained many friends, who all said he was a rare one, a true cavalier; and that pleased the soldier well. But as he spent money every day and never earned any, he had at last only two shillings left; and he was obliged to turn out of the fine rooms in which he had dwelt, and had to live in a little garret under the roof, and clean his boots for himself, and mend them with a darning-needle. None of his friends came to see him, for there were too many stairs to climb.

It was quite dark one evening, and he could not even buy himself a candle, when it occurred to him that there was a candle-end in the tinder box which he had taken out of the hollow tree into which the witch had helped him. He brought out the tinder box and the candle-end; but as soon as he struck fire and the sparks rose up from the flint, the door flew open, and the dog who had eyes as big as a couple of teacups, and whom he had seen in the tree, stood before him, and said,

"What are my lord's commands?"

"What is this?" said the soldier. "That's a famous tinder box, if I can get everything with it that I want! Bring me some money," said he to the dog; and *whisk!* the dog was gone, and *whisk!* he was back again, with a great bagful of shillings in his mouth.

Now the soldier knew what a capital tinder box this was. If he struck it once, the dog came who sat upon the chest of copper money; if he struck it twice, the dog came who had the silver; and if he struck it three times, then appeared the dog who had the gold. Now the soldier moved back into the fine rooms, and appeared again in handsome clothes; and all his friends knew him again, and cared very much for him indeed.

Once he thought to himself, "It is a very strange thing that one cannot get to see the princess. They all say she is very beautiful; but what is the use of that, if she has always to sit in the great copper castle with the many towers? Can I not get to see her at all? Where is my tinder box?" And so he struck a light, and *whisk!* came the dog with eyes as big as teacups.

"It is midnight, certainly," said the soldier, "but I should very much like to see the princes only for one little moment."

The dog was outside the door directly, and, before the soldier thought it, came back with the princess. She sat upon the dog's back and slept; and every one could see she was a real princess, for she was so lovely. The soldier could not refrain from kissing her, for he was a thorough soldier. Then the dog ran back again with the princess. But when morning came, and the king and queen were drinking tea, the princess said she had had a strange dream the night before, about a dog and a soldier—that she had ridden upon the dog, and the soldier had kissed her.

"That would be a fine history!" said the Queen.

So one of the old court ladies had to watch the next night by the princess's bed, to see if this was really a dream, or what it might be.

The soldier had a great longing to see the lovely princess again; so the dog came in the night, took her away, and ran as fast as he could. But the old lady put on water-

7

boots, and ran just as fast after him. When she saw that they both entered a great house, she thought, "Now I know where it is"; and with a bit of chalk she drew a great cross on the door. Then she went home and lay down, and the dog came up with the princess; but when he saw that there was a cross drawn on the door where the soldier lived, he took a piece of chalk, too, and drew crosses on all the doors in the town. And that was cleverly done, for now the lady could not find the right door, because all the doors had crosses upon them.

In the morning early came the King and the Queen, the old court lady and all the officers, to see where it was the princess had been. "Here it is!" said the King, when he saw the first door with a cross upon it. "No, my dear husband, it is there!" said the Queen, who descried another door which also showed a cross. "But *there* is one, and *there* is one!" said all, for wherever they looked there were crosses on the doors. So they saw that it would avail them nothing if they searched on.

But the Queen was an exceedingly clever woman, who could do more than ride in a coach. She took her great gold scissors, cut a piece of silk into pieces, and made a neat little bag; this bag she filled with fine wheat flour, and tied it on the princess's back; and when that was done, she cut a little hole in the bag, so that the flour would be scattered along all the way which the princess should take.

In the night the dog came again, took the princess on his back, and ran with her to the soldier, who loved her very much, and would gladly have been a prince, so that he might have married her. The dog did not notice at all how the flour ran out in a stream from the castle to the windows of the soldier's house, where he ran up the wall with the princess. In the morning the King and the Queen saw well enough where their daughter had been, and they took the soldier and put him in prison.

There he sat. Oh, but it was dark and disagreeable there! And they said to him, "To-morrow you shall be hanged." That was not amusing to hear, and he had left his tinder box at the inn. In the morning he could see, through the iron grating of the little window, how the people were hurrying out of the town to see him hanged. He heard the drums beat and saw the soldiers marching. All the people were running out, and among them was a shoemaker's boy with leather apron and slippers, and he galloped so fast that one of his slippers flew off, and came right against the wall where the soldier sat looking through the iron grating.

"Halloo, you shoemaker's boy! you needn't be in such a hurry," cried the soldier to him: "it will not begin till I come. But if you will run to where I lived, and bring me my tinder box, you shall have four shillings; but you must put your best leg foremost."

The shoemaker's boy wanted to get the four shillings, so

he went and brought the tinder box, and—well, we shall hear now what happened.

Outside the town a great gallows had been built, and round it stood the soldiers and many hundred thousand people. The King and Queen sat on a splendid throne, opposite to the judges and the whole council. The soldier already stood upon the ladder; but as they were about to put the rope round his neck, he said that before a poor criminal suffered his punishment an innocent request was always granted to him. He wanted very much to smoke a pipe of tobacco, and it would be the last pipe he should smoke in the world. The king would not say "No" to this; so the soldier took his tinder box, and struck fire. One—two—three!—and there suddenly stood all the dogs—the one with eyes as big as teacups, the one with eyes as large as mill-wheels, and the one whose eyes were as big as the round tower.

"Help me now, so that I may not be hanged," said the soldier. And the dogs fell upon the judge and all the council, seized one by the leg and another by the nose, and tossed them all many feet into the air, so that they fell down and were all broken to pieces.

"I won't!" cried the King; but the biggest dog took him and the Queen, and threw them after the others. Then the soldiers were afraid, and the people cried, "Little soldier, you shall be our king, and marry the beautiful princess!"

So they put the soldier into the king's coach, and all

the three dogs danced in front and cried "Hurrah!" and the boys whistled through their fingers, and the soldiers presented arms. The princess came out of the copper castle, and became queen, and she liked that well enough. The wedding lasted a week, and the three dogs sat at the table too and opened their eyes wider than ever at all they saw.

GREAT · CLAUS · AND · LITTLE · CLAUS

GREAT CLAUS AND LITTLE CLAUS

HERE lived two men in one village, and they had the same name—each was called Claus; but one had four horses, and the other only a single horse. To distinguish them from each other, folks called him who had four horses Great Claus, and the one who had only a single horse Little Claus. Now we shall hear what happened to each of them, for this is a true story.

The whole week through Little Claus was obliged to plough for Great Claus, and to lend him his one horse; then Great Claus helped him out with all his four, but only once a week and that was on Sunday. Hurrah! how Little Claus smacked his whip over all five horses, for they were as good as his own on that one day. The sun shone gaily, and all the bells in the steeples were ringing; the people were all dressed in their best, and were going to church, with their hymn-books under their arms, to hear the clergyman preach,

and they saw Little Claus ploughing with five horses; but he was so merry that he smacked his whip again and again, and cried, "Gee up, all my five!"

"You must not talk so," said Great Claus, "for only one horse is yours."

But when any one passed Little Claus forgot that he was not to say this, and he cried, "Gee up, all my horses!"

"Now I must beg of you to stop that," cried Great Claus, "for if you say it again, I shall hit your horse on the head, so that it will fall down dead, and then it will be all over with him."

"I will certainly not say it any more," said Little Claus.

But when people came by soon afterwards, and nodded "good day" to him, he became very glad, and thought it looked very well, after all, that he had five horses to plough his field; and so he smacked his whip again, and cried, "Gee up, all my horses!"

"I'll 'gee up' your horses!" said Great Claus. And he took a mallet and hit the only horse of Little Claus on the head, so that it fell down, and was dead immediately.

"Oh, now I haven't any horse at all!" said Little Claus, and began to cry.

Then he flayed the horse, and let the hide dry in the wind, and put it in a sack and hung it over his shoulder, and went to town to sell his horse's skin.

He had a very long way to go, and was obliged to pass

through a great dark wood, and the weather became dreadfully bad. He went quite astray, and before he got into the right way again it was evening, and it was too far to get home again or even to the town before nightfall.

Close by the road stood a large farm-house. The shutters were closed outside the windows, but the light could still be seen shining out over them.

"I may be able to get leave to stop here through the night," thought Little Claus; and he went and knocked.

The farmer's wife opened the door; but when she heard what he wanted she told him to go away, declaring that her husband was not at home, and she would not receive strangers.

"Then I shall have to lie outside," said Little Claus. And the farmer's wife shut the door in his face.

Close by stood a great haystack, and between this and the farm-house was a little outhouse thatched with straw.

"Up there I can lie," said Little Claus, when he looked up at the roof; "that is a capital bed. I suppose the stork won't fly down and bite me in the legs." For a living stork was standing on the roof where he had his nest.

Now Little Claus climbed up to the roof of the shed, where he lay, and turned round to settle himself comfortably. The wooden shutters did not cover the windows at the top, and he could look straight into the room. There was a great table, with the cloth laid, and wine and roast meat and a glorious fish upon it. The farmer's wife and

the parish clerk were seated at table, and nobody besides. She was filling his glass, and he was digging his fork into the fish, for that was his favourite dish.

"If one could only get some too!" thought Little Claus, as he stretched out his head towards the window. Heavens! what a glorious cake he saw standing there! Yes, certainly, that *was* a feast.

Now he heard some one riding along the high road. It was the woman's husband, who was coming home. He was a good man enough, but he had the strange peculiarity that he could never bear to see a clerk. If a clerk appeared before his eyes he became quite wild. And that was the reason why the clerk had gone to the wife to wish her good day, because he knew that her husband was not at home; and the good woman therefore put the best fare she had before him. But when they heard the man coming they were frightened, and the woman begged the clerk to creep into a great empty chest which stood in the corner; and he did so, for he knew the husband could not bear the sight of a clerk. The woman quickly hid all the excellent meat and wine in her baking-oven; for if the man had seen that, he would have been certain to ask what it meant.

"Oh, dear!" sighed Little Claus, up in his shed, when he saw all the good fare put away.

"Is there any one up there?" asked the farmer; and he looked up at Little Claus. "Why are you lying there? Better come with me into the room."

And Little Claus told him how he had lost his way, and asked leave to stay there for the night.

"Yes, certainly," said the peasant, "but first we must have something to live on."

The woman received them both in a friendly way, spread the cloth on a long table, and gave them a great dish of porridge. The farmer was hungry, and ate with a good appetite; but Little Claus could not help thinking of the capital roast meat, fish, and cake, which he knew were in the oven. Under the table, at his feet, he had laid the sack with the horse's hide in it; for we know that he had come out to sell it in the town. He could not relish the porridge, so he trod on the sack, and the dry skin inside crackled quite loudly.

"Hush," said Little Claus to his sack; but at the same time he trod on it again, so that it crackled much louder than before.

"Why, what have you got in your sack?" asked the farmer.

"Oh, that's a magician," answered Little Claus. "He says we are not to eat porridge, for he has conjured the oven full of roast meat, fish, and cake."

"Wonderful!" cried the farmer; and he opened the oven in a hurry, and found all the dainty provisions which his wife had hidden there, but which, as he thought, the wizard had conjured forth. The woman dared not say anything, but put the things at once on the table; and so they both

19

ate of the meat, the fish and the cake. Now Little Claus again trod on his sack, and made the hide creak.

"What does he say now?" said the farmer.

"He says," replied Claus, "that he has conjured three bottles of wine for us, too, and that they are also standing there in the oven."

Now the woman was obliged to bring out the wine which she had hidden, and the farmer drank it and became very merry. He would have been very glad to own such a conjurer as Little Claus had there in the sack.

"Can he conjure the demon forth?" asked the farmer. "I should like to see him, for now I am merry."

"Oh, yes," said Little Claus, "my conjurer can do anything that I ask of him.—Can you not?" he added, and trod on the hide, so that it crackled. "He says 'Yes.' But the demon is very ugly to look at: we had better not see him."

"Oh, I'm not at all afraid. Pray, what will he look like?"

"Why, he'll look the very image of a parish-clerk."

"Ha!" said the farmer, "that *is* ugly! You must know, I can't bear the sight of a clerk. But it doesn't matter now, for I know that he's a demon, so I shall easily stand it. Now I have courage, but he must not come too near me."

"Now I will ask my conjurer," said Little Claus; and he trod on the sack and held his ear down.

"What does he say?"

"He says you may go and open the chest that stands in

the corner, and you will see the demon crouching in it; but you must hold the lid so that he doesn't slip out."

"Will you help me to hold him?" asked the farmer. And he went to the chest where the wife had hidden the real clerk, who sat in there and was very much afraid. The farmer opened the lid a little way and peeped in underneath it.

"Ugh!" he cried, and sprang backward. "Yes, now I've seen him, and he looked exactly like our clerk. Oh! that was dreadful!"

Upon this they must drink. So they sat and drank until late into the night.

"You must sell me that conjurer," said the farmer. "Ask as much as you like for him: I'll give you a whole bushel of money directly."

"No, that I can't do," said Little Claus: "only think how much use I can make of this conjurer."

"Oh, I should so much like to have him!" cried the farmer; and he went on begging.

"Well," said Little Claus, at last, "as you have been so kind as to give me shelter for the night, I will let it be so. You shall have the conjurer for a bushel of money; but I must have the bushel heaped up."

"That you shall have," replied the farmer. "But you must take the chest yonder away with you. I will not keep it in my house an hour. One cannot know—perhaps he may be there still."

GREAT CLAUS AND LITTLE CLAUS

Little Claus gave the farmer his sack with the dry hide in it, and got in exchange a whole bushel of money, and that heaped up. The farmer also gave him a big truck, on which to carry off his money and chest.

"Farewell!" said Little Claus; and he went off with his money and the big chest, in which the clerk was still sitting.

On the other side of the wood was a great deep river. The water rushed along so rapidly that one could scarcely swim against the stream. A fine new bridge had been built over it. Little Claus stopped on the centre of the bridge, and said quite loud, so that the clerk could hear it, "Ho, what shall I do with this stupid chest? It's as heavy as if stones were in it. I shall only get tired if I drag it any farther, so I'll throw it into the river: if it swims home to me, well and good; and if it does not it will be no great matter."

And he took the chest with one hand, and lifted it up a little, as if he intended to throw it into the river.

"No! let be!" cried the clerk from within the chest; "let me out first!"

"Ugh!" exclaimed Little Claus, pretending to be frightened, "he's in there still! I must make haste and throw him into the river, that he may be drowned."

"Oh, no, no!" screamed the clerk. "I'll give you a whole bushelful of money if you'll let me go."

"Why, that's another thing!" said Little Claus; and he opened the chest.

22

The clerk crept quickly out, pushed the empty chest into the water, and went to his house, where Little Claus received a whole bushelful of money. He had already received one from the farmer, and so now he had his truck loaded with money.

"See, I've been paid well for the horse," he said to himself when he had got home to his own room, and was emptying all the money into a heap in the middle of the floor. "That will vex Great Claus when he hears how rich I have grown through my one horse; but I won't tell him about it outright."

So he sent a boy to Great Claus to ask for a bushel measure.

"What can he want with it?" thought Great Claus. And he smeared some tar underneath the measure, so that some part of whatever was measured should stick to it. And thus it happened; for when he received the measure back, there were three new threepenny pieces adhering thereto.

"What is this?" cried Great Claus; and he ran off at once to Little Claus. "Where did you get all that money from?"

"Oh, that's for my horse's skin. I sold it yesterday evening."

"That's really being well paid," said Great Claus. And he ran home in a hurry, took an axe, and killed all his four horses; then he flayed them, and carried off their skins to the town.

23

"Hides! hides! who'll buy any hides?" he cried through the streets.

All the shoemakers and tanners came running, and asked how much he wanted for them.

"A bushel of money for each!" said Great Claus.

"Are you mad?" said they. "Do you think we have money by the bushel?"

"Hides! hides!" he cried again; and to all who asked him what the hides would cost he replied, "A bushel of money."

"He wants to make fools of us," they all exclaimed. And the shoemakers took their straps, and the tanners their aprons, and they began to beat Great Claus.

"Hides! hides!" they called after him, jeeringly. "Yes, we'll tan your hide for you till the red broth runs down. Out of the town with him!" And Great Claus made the best haste he could, for he had never yet been thrashed as he was thrashed now.

"Well," said he when he got home, "Little Claus shall pay for this. I'll kill him for it."

Now, at Little Claus's the old grandmother had died. She had been very harsh and unkind to him, but yet he was very sorry, and took the dead woman and laid her in his warm bed, to see if she would not come back to life again. There he intended she should remain all through the night, and he himself would sit in the corner and sleep on a chair as he had often done before. As he sat there,

24

in the night the door opened, and Great Claus came in with his axe. He knew where Little Claus's bed stood; and, going straight up to it, he hit the old grandmother on the head, thinking she was Little Claus.

"D'ye see," said he, "you shall not make a fool of me again." And then he went home.

"That's a bad fellow, that man," said Little Claus. "He wanted to kill me. It was a good thing for my old grandmother that she was dead already. He would have taken her life."

And he dressed his grandmother in her Sunday clothes, borrowed a horse of his neighbour, harnessed it to a car, and put the old lady on the back seat, so that she could not fall out when he drove. And so they trundled through the wood. When the sun rose they were in front of an inn; there Little Claus pulled up, and went in to have some refreshment.

The host had very, very much money; he was also a very good man, but exceedingly hot-tempered, as if he had pepper and tobacco in him.

"Good-morning," said he to Little Claus. "You've put on your Sunday clothes early to-day."

"Yes," answered Little Claus; "I'm going to town with my old grandmother: she's sitting there on the car without. I can't bring her into the room—will you give her a glass of mead? But you must speak very loud for she can't hear well."

"Yes, that I will," said the host. And he poured out a great glass of mead, and went out with it to the dead grandmother, who had been placed upright in the carriage.

"Here's a glass of mead from your son," quoth mine host. But the dead woman replied not a word, but sat quite still. "Don't you hear?" cried the host as loud as he could, "here is a glass of mead from your son!"

Once more he called out the same thing, but as she still made not a movement, he became angry at last, and threw the glass in her face, so that the mead ran down over her nose, and she tumbled backwards into the car, for she had only been put upright, and not bound fast.

"Hallo!" cried Little Claus, running out at the door and seizing the host by the breast; "you've killed my grandmother now! See, there's a big hole in her forehead."

"Oh, here's a misfortune!" cried the host, wringing his hands. "That all comes of my hot temper. Dear Little Claus, I'll give you a bushel of money, and have your grandmother buried as if she were my own; only keep quiet, or I shall have my head cut off, and that would be so very disagreeable!"

So Little Claus again received a whole bushel of money, and the host buried the old grandmother, as if she had been his own. And when Little Claus came home with all his money, he at once sent his boy to Great Claus to ask to borrow a bushel measure.

"What's that?" said Great Claus. "Have I not killed

him? I must go myself and see to this." And so he went over himself with the bushel to Little Claus.

"Now, where did you get all that money from?" he asked; and he opened his eyes wide when he saw all that had been brought together.

"You killed my grandmother, and not me," replied Little Claus; "and I've been and sold her, and got a whole bushel of money for her."

"That's really being well paid," said Great Claus; and he hastened home, took an axe, and killed his own grandmother directly. Then he put her on a carriage, and drove off to the town with her, to where the apothecary lived, and asked him if he would buy a dead person.

"Who is it, and where did you get him from?" asked the apothecary.

"It's my grandmother," answered Great Claus. "I've killed her to get a bushel of money for her."

"Heaven save us!" cried the apothecary, "you're raving! Don't say such things or you may lose your head." And he told him earnestly what a bad deed this was that he had done, and what a bad man he was, and that he must be punished. And Great Claus was so frightened that he jumped out of the surgery straight into his carriage, and whipped the horses and drove home. But the apothecary and all the people thought him mad, and so they let him drive whither he would.

"You shall pay for this!" said Great Claus, when he

was out upon the high road: "yes, you shall pay me for this, Little Claus!" And directly he got home he took the biggest sack he could find and went over to Little Claus and said, "Now, you've tricked me again! First I killed my horses, and then my old grandmother! That's all your fault; but you shall never trick me any more." And he seized Little Claus round the body, and thrust him into the sack, and took him upon his back, and called out to him, "Now I shall go off with you and drown you."

It was a long way that he had to travel before he came to the river, and Little Claus was not too light to carry. The road led him close to a church: the organ was playing, and the people singing so beautifully! Then Great Claus put down his sack, with Little Claus in it, close to the church door and thought it would be a very good thing to go in and hear a psalm before he went farther; for Little Claus could not get out, and all the people were in church; and so he went in.

"Oh, dear! Oh, dear!" sighed Little Claus in the sack. And he turned and twisted, but he found it impossible to loosen the cord. Then there came by an old drover with snow-white hair, and a great staff in his hand; he was driving a whole herd of cows and oxen before him, and they stumbled against the sack in which Little Claus was confined, so it was overthrown.

"Oh, dear!" sighed Little Claus, "I'm so young yet, and am to go to heaven directly?"

"And I, poor fellow," said the drover, "am so old already, and can't get there yet!"

"Open the sack," cried Little Claus; "creep into it instead of me, and you will get to heaven directly."

"With all my heart," replied the drover; and he untied the sack, out of which Little Claus crept forth immediately.

"But will you look after the cattle?" said the old man; and he crept into the sack at once, whereupon Little Claus tied it up and went his way with all the cows and oxen.

Soon afterwards Great Claus came out of the church. He took the sack on his shoulders again, although it seemed to him as if the sack had become lighter; for the old drover was only half as heavy as Little Claus.

"How light he is to carry now! Yes, that is because I have heard a psalm."

So he went to the river, which was deep and broad, threw the sack with the old drover in it into the water, and called after him, thinking that it was Little Claus, "You lie there! Now you shan't trick me any more!"

Then he went home; but when he came to a place where there was a cross-road, he met Little Claus driving all his beasts.

"What's this?" cried Great Claus. "Have I not drowned you?"

"Yes," replied Little Claus, "you threw me into the river less than half an hour ago."

"But wherever did you get all those fine beasts from?" asked Great Claus.

"These beasts are sea-cattle," replied Little Claus. "I'll tell you the whole story,—and thank you for drowning me, for now I'm at the top of the tree. I am really rich! How frightened I was when I lay huddled in the sack, and the wind whistled about my ears when you threw me down from the bridge into the cold water! I sank to the bottom immediately; but I did not knock myself, for the most splendid soft grass grows down there. Upon that I fell; and immediately the sack was opened, and the loveliest maiden, with snow-white garments and a green wreath upon her wet hair, took me by the hand, and said, 'Are you come, Little Claus? Here you have some cattle to begin with. A mile further along the road there is a whole herd more, which I will give to you.' And now I saw that the river formed a great highway for the people of the sea. Down in its bed they walked and drove directly from the sea, and straight into the land, to where the river ends. There it was so beautifully full of flowers and of the freshest grass; the fishes which swam in the water shot past my ears, just as here the birds in the air. What pretty people there were there, and what fine cattle pasturing on mounds and in ditches!"

"But why did you come up again to us directly?" asked Great Claus. "I should not have done that, if it is so beautiful down there."

"Why," replied Little Claus, "just in that I acted with good policy. You heard me tell you that the sea-maiden said, 'A mile farther along the road'—and by the road she meant the river, for she can't go anywhere else—'there is a whole herd of cattle for you.' But I know what bends the stream makes—sometimes this way, sometimes that; there's a long way to go round: no, the thing can be managed in a shorter way by coming here to the land, and driving across the fields towards the river again. In this manner I save myself almost half a mile, and get all the quicker to my sea-cattle!"

"Oh, you are a fortunate man!" said Great Claus. "Do you think I should get some sea-cattle too if I went down to the bottom of the river?"

"Yes, I think so," replied Little Claus. "But I cannot carry you in the sack as far as the river; you are too heavy for me! But if you will go there, and creep into the sack yourself, I will throw you in with a great deal of pleasure."

"Thanks!" said Great Claus; "but if I don't get any sea-cattle when I am down there, I shall beat you, you may be sure!"

"Oh, no; don't be so fierce!"

And so they went together to the river. When the beasts, which were thirsty, saw the stream, they ran as fast as they could to get at the water.

"See how they hurry!" cried Little Claus. "They are longing to get back to the bottom."

"Yes, but help me first!" said Great Claus, "or else you shall be beaten."

And so he crept into the great sack, which had been laid across the back of one of the oxen.

"Put a stone in, for I'm afraid I shan't sink else," said Great Claus.

"That will be all right," replied Little Claus; and he put a big stone into the sack, tied the rope tightly, and pushed against it. *Plump!* There lay Great Claus in the river, and sank at once to the bottom.

"I'm afraid he won't find the cattle!" said Little Claus; and then he drove homeward with what he had.

THE·REAL·PRINCESS

THE REAL PRINCESS

 NCE there was a Prince who wished to marry a Princess; but then she must be a real Princess. He travelled all over the world in hopes of finding such a lady; but there was always something wrong. Princesses he found in plenty; but whether they were real Princesses it was impossible for him to decide, for now one thing, now another, seemed to him not quite right about the ladies. At last he returned to his palace quite cast down, because he wished so much to have a real Princess for his wife.

One evening a fearful tempest arose; it thundered and lightened, and the rain poured down from the sky in torrents; besides, it was as dark as pitch. All at once there was heard a violent knocking at the door, and the old King, the Prince's father, went out himself to open it.

It was a Princess who was standing outside the door. What with the rain and the wind, she was in a sad condition: the water trickled down from her hair, and her clothes clung to her body. She said she was a real Princess.

THE REAL PRINCESS

"Ah, we shall soon see that!" thought the old Queen-mother; however, she said not a word of what she was going to do, but went quietly into the bedroom, took all the bed-clothes off the bed, and put three little peas on the bedstead. She then laid twenty mattresses one upon another over the three peas, and put twenty feather-beds over the mattresses.

Upon this bed the Princess was to pass the night.

The next morning she was asked how she had slept. "Oh, very badly indeed!" she replied. "I have scarcely closed my eyes the whole night through. I do not know what was in my bed, but I had something hard under me, and am all over black and blue. It has hurt me so much!"

Now it was plain that the lady must be a real Princess, since she had been able to feel the three little peas through the twenty mattresses and twenty feather-beds. None but a real Princess could have had such a delicate sense of feeling.

The Prince accordingly made her his wife, being now convinced that he had found a real Princess. The three peas were, however, put into the cabinet of curiosities, where they are still to be seen, provided they are not lost.

Was not this a lady of real delicacy?

THE · HARDY · TIN · SOLDIER

THE HARDY TIN SOLDIER

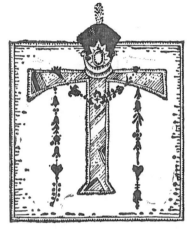HERE were once five and twenty tin soldiers; they were all brothers, for they had all been born of one old tin spoon. They shouldered their muskets, and looked straight before them: their uniform was red and blue, and very splendid. The first thing they had heard in the world, when the lid was taken off their box, had been the words "Tin Soldiers!" These words were uttered by a little boy, clapping his hands: the soldiers had been given to him, for it was his birthday; and now he put them upon the table. Each soldier was exactly like the rest only one of them was a little different, he had but one leg, for he had been cast last of all, and there had not been enough tin to finish him; but he stood as firmly upon his one leg as the others on their two; and it was just this soldier who became remarkable.

On the table on which they had been placed stood many other playthings, but the toy that attracted most attention was a neat castle of cardboard. Through the little windows one could see straight into the hall. Before the castle some little trees were placed round a little looking-glass, which

was to represent a clear lake. Waxen swans swam on this lake and were mirrored in it. This was all very pretty; but the prettiest of all was a little lady, who stood at the open door of the castle: she was also cut out in paper, but she had a dress of the clearest gauze, and a little narrow blue ribbon over her shoulders, that looked like a scarf; and in the middle of this ribbon was a shining tinsel rose as big as her whole face. The little lady stretched out both her arms, for she was a dancer; and then she lifted one leg so high that the tin soldier could not see it at all, and thought that, like himself, she had but one leg.

"That would be the wife for me," thought he; "but she is very grand. She lives in a castle, and I have only a box, and there are five and twenty of us in that. It is no place for her. But I must try to make acquaintance with her."

And then he lay down at full length behind a snuff-box which was on the table; there he could easily watch the little dainty lady, who continued to stand on one leg without losing her balance.

When the evening came, all the other tin soldiers were put into their box, and the people in the house went to bed. Now the toys began to play at "visiting," and at "war" and "giving balls." The tin soldiers rattled in their box, for they wanted to join, but could not lift the lid. The nutcracker threw somersaults, and the pencil amused itself on the table: there was so much noise that the canary woke up, and began to speak too, and even in verse. The only

"*Oh, very badly indeed!*" *she replied.* "*I have scarcely closed my eyes the whole night through. I do not know what was in my bed.*"

[See Page 36]

two who did not stir from their places were the tin soldier and the dancing lady: she stood straight up on the point of one of her toes, and stretched out both her arms; and he was just as enduring on his one leg; and he never turned his eyes away from her.

Now the clock struck twelve—and, bounce!—the lid flew off the snuff-box; but there was not snuff in it, but a little black goblin: you see it was a trick.

"Tin soldier!" said the goblin, "will you keep your eyes to yourself?"

But the tin soldier pretended not to hear him.

"Just you wait until to-morrow!" said the goblin.

But when morning came, and the children got up, the tin soldier was placed in the window; and whether it was the goblin or the draught that did it, all at once the window flew open, and the soldier fell head over heels out of the third story. That was a terrible passage! He put his leg straight up, and stuck with his helmet downwards and his bayonet between the paving-stones.

The servant-maid and the little boy came down directly to look for him, but though they almost trod upon him they could not see him. If the soldier had cried out "Here I am!" they would have found him; but he did not think it fitting to call out loudly because he was in uniform.

Now it began to rain; the drops soon fell thicker, and at last it came down in a complete stream. When the rain was past, two street boys came by.

THE HARDY TIN SOLDIER

"Just look!" said one of them, "there lies a tin soldier. He shall go out sailing."

And they made a boat out of a newspaper, and put the tin soldier in the middle of it; and so he sailed down the gutter, and the two boys ran beside him and clapped their hands. Goodness preserve us! how the waves rose in that gutter, and how fast the stream ran! But then it had been a heavy rain. The paper boat rocked up and down, and sometimes turned round so rapidly that the tin soldier trembled; but he remained firm, and never changed countenance, but looked straight before him, and shouldered his musket.

All at once the boat went into a long drain, and it became as dark as if he had been in his box.

"Where am I going now?" he thought. "Yes, yes, that's the goblin's fault. Ah! if the little lady only sat here with me in the boat, it might be twice as dark for what I should care."

Suddenly there came a great water-rat, which lived under the drain.

"Have you a passport?" said the rat. "Give me your passport."

But the tin soldier kept silence, and held his musket tighter than ever.

The boat went on, but the rat came after it. Ugh! how he gnashed his teeth, and called out to the bits of straw and wood.

"Hold him! hold him! he hasn't paid toll—he hasn't shown his passport!"

But the stream became stronger and stronger. The tin soldier could see the bright daylight where the arch ended; but he heard a roaring noise, which might well frighten a bolder man. Only think—just where the tunnel ended, the drain ran into a great canal; and for him that would have been as dangerous as for us to be carried down a great waterfall.

Now he was already so near it that he could not stop. The boat was carried out, the poor tin soldier stiffening himself as much as he could, and no one could say that he moved an eyelid. The boat whirled round three or four times, and was full of water to the very edge—it must sink. The tin soldier stood up to his neck in water, and the boat sank deeper and deeper, and the paper was loosened more and more; and now the water closed over the soldier's head. Then he thought of the pretty little dancer, and how he should never see her again; and it sounded in the soldier's ears:

> Farewell, farewell, thou warrior brave,
> For this day thou must die!

And now the paper parted, and the tin soldier fell out; but at that moment he was snapped up by a great fish.

Oh, how dark it was in that fish's body! It was darker yet than in the drain tunnel; and then it was very narrow

45

too. But the tin soldier remained unmoved, and lay at full length shouldering his musket.

The fish swam to and fro; he made the most wonderful movements, and then became quite still. At last something flashed through him like lightning. The daylight shone quite clear, and a voice said aloud, "The tin soldier!" The fish had been caught, carried to market, bought, and taken into the kitchen, where the cook cut him open with a large knife. She seized the soldier round the body with both her hands, and carried him into the room, where all were anxious to see the remarkable man who had travelled about in the inside of a fish; but the tin soldier was not at all proud. They placed him on the table, and there—no! What curious things may happen in the world! The tin soldier was in the very room in which he had been before! he saw the same children, and the same toys stood on the table; and there was the pretty castle with the graceful little dancer. She was still balancing herself on one leg, and held the other extended in the air. She was hardy too. That moved the tin soldier: he was very nearly weeping tin tears, but that would not have been proper. He looked at her and she at him, but they said nothing to each other.

Then one of the little boys took the tin soldier and flung him into the stove. He gave no reason for doing this. It must have been the fault of the goblin in the snuff-box.

The tin soldier stood there quite illuminated, and felt a

The draught of air caught the dancer, and
she flew like a sylph just into the
stove to the tin soldier.

[See Page 49]

heat that was terrible; but whether this heat proceeded from the real fire or from love he did not know. The colours had quite gone off from him; but whether that had happened on the journey, or had been caused by grief, no one could say. He looked at the little lady, she looked at him and he felt that he was melting; but he still stood firm, shouldering his musket. Then suddenly the door flew open, and the draught of air caught the dancer, and she flew like a sylph just into the stove to the tin soldier, and flashed up into a flame, and she was gone. Then the tin soldier melted down into a lump, and when the servant-maid took the ashes out next day, she found him in the shape of a little tin heart. But of the dancer nothing remained but the tinsel rose, and that was burned as black as a coal.

THE · FLYING · TRUNK

THE FLYING TRUNK

THERE was once a merchant, who was so rich that he could pave the whole street with silver coins, and almost have enough left for a little lane. But he did not do that; he knew how to employ his money differently. When he spent a shilling he got back a crown, such a clever merchant was he; and this continued till he died.

His son now got all this money; and he lived merrily, going to the masquerade every evening, making kites out of dollar notes, and playing at ducks and drakes on the sea coast with gold pieces instead of pebbles. In this way the money might soon be spent, and indeed it was so. At last he had no more than four shillings left, and no clothes to wear but a pair of slippers and an old dressing-gown. Now his friends did not trouble themselves any more about him, as they could not walk with him in the street; but one of them, who was good-natured, sent him an old trunk, with the remark, "Pack up!" Yes, that was all very well, but he had nothing to pack, therefore he seated himself in the trunk.

That was a wonderful trunk. So soon as any one pressed the lock the trunk could fly. This it now did; *whirr!* away it flew with him through the chimney and over the clouds, farther and farther away. But as often as the bottom of the trunk cracked a little he was in great fear lest it might go to pieces, and then he would have thrown a fine somersault! In that way he came to the land of the Turks. He hid the trunk in a wood under some dry leaves, and then went into the town. He could do that very well, for among the Turks all the people went dressed like himself in dressing-gown and slippers. Then he met a nurse with a little child.

"Here, you Turkish nurse," he began, "what kind of a great castle is that close by the town, in which the windows are so high up?"

"There dwells the Sultan's daughter," replied she. "It is prophesied that she will be very unhappy respecting a lover; and therefore nobody may go to her, unless the Sultan and Sultana are there too."

"Thank you!" said the merchant's son; and he went out into the forest, seated himself in his trunk, flew on the roof, and crept through the window into the Princess's room.

She was lying asleep on the sofa, and she was so beautiful that the merchant's son was compelled to kiss her. Then she awoke, and was very much startled; but he said he was a Turkish angel who had come down to her through the air, and that pleased her.

They sat down side by side, and he told her stories about her eyes; he told her they were the most glorious dark lakes, and that thoughts were swimming about in them like mermaids. And he told her about her forehead; that it was a snowy mountain with the most splendid halls and pictures. And he told her about the stork who brings the lovely little children.

Yes, those were fine histories! Then he asked the Princess if she would marry him, and she said "Yes," directly.

"But you must come here on Saturday," said she. "Then the Sultan and the Sultana will be here to tea. They will be very proud that I am to marry a Turkish angel. But take care that you know a very pretty story, for both my parents are very fond indeed of stories. My mother likes them high-flown and moral, but my father likes them merry so that one can laugh."

"Yes, I shall bring no marriage gift but a story," said he; and so they parted. But the Princess gave him a sabre, the sheath embroidered with gold pieces, and that was very useful to him.

Now he flew away, bought a new dressing-gown, and sat in the forest and made up a story; it was to be ready by Saturday, and that was not an easy thing.

By the time he had finished it Saturday had come. The

Sultan and his wife and all the court were at the Princess's to tea. He was received very graciously.

"Will you tell us a story?" said the Sultana; "one that is deep and edifying."

"Yes, but one that we can laugh at," said the Sultan.

"Certainly," he replied; and began. And now listen well.

"There was once a bundle of Matches, and these Matches were particularly proud of their high descent. Their genealogical tree, that is to say, the great fir tree of which each of them was a little splinter, had been a great old tree out in the forest. The Matches now lay between a Tinder-box and an old iron Pot; and they were telling about the days of their youth. 'Yes, when we were upon the green boughs,' they said, 'then we really were upon the green boughs! Every morning and evening there was diamond tea for us, I mean dew; we had sunshine all day long whenever the sun shone, and all the little birds had to tell stories. We could see very well that we were rich, for the other trees were only dressed out in summer, while our family had the means to wear green dresses in the winter as well. But then the woodcutter came, like a great revolution, and our family was broken up. The head of the family got an appointment as mainmast in a first-rate ship, which could sail round the world if necessary; the other branches went to other places, and now we have the office of kindling a

56

light for the vulgar herd. That's how we grand people came to be in the kitchen.'

" 'My fate was of a different kind,' said the iron Pot which stood next to the Matches. 'From the beginning ever since I came into the world, there has been a great deal of scouring and cooking done in me. I look after the practical part, and am the first here in the house. My only pleasure is to sit in my place after dinner, very clean and neat, and to carry on a sensible conversation with my comrades. But except the Water Pot, which sometimes is taken down into the courtyard, we always live within our four walls. Our only newsmonger is the Market Basket; but he speaks very uneasily about the government and the people. Yes, the other day there was an old pot that fell down from fright, and burst. He's liberal, I can tell you!' 'Now you're talking too much,' the Tinder-box interrupted, and the Steel struck against the Flint, so that sparks flew out. 'Shall we not have a merry evening?'

" 'Yes, let us talk about who is the grandest,' said the Matches.

" 'No, I don't like to talk about myself,' retorted the Pot. 'Let us get up an evening entertainment. I will begin. I will tell a story from real life, something that every one has experienced, so that we can easily imagine the situation, and take pleasure in it. On the Baltic, by the Danish beech-trees——'

THE FLYING TRUNK

" 'That's a pretty beginning!' cried all the Plates. 'That will be a story we shall like.'

" 'Yes, there I spent my youth in a quiet family where the furniture was polished, and the floors scoured, and new curtains were put up every fortnight.'

" 'What an interesting way you have of telling a story!' said the Carpet Broom. 'One can tell directly that the narrator is a woman. There's something pure runs through it.'

" 'Yes, one feels that,' said the Water Pot, and out of delight it gave a little hop, so that there was a splash on the floor.

"And the Pot went on telling her story, and the end was as good as the beginning.

"All the Plates rattled with joy, and the Carpet Broom brought some green parsley out of the dust hole, and put it like a wreath on the Pot, for he knew that it would vex the others. 'If I crown her to-day,' it thought, 'she will crown me to-morrow.'

" 'Now I'll dance,' said the Fire Tongs, and she danced. Preserve us! how that implement could lift up one leg! The old Chair Cushion burst to see it. 'Shall I be crowned too?' thought the Tongs; and indeed a wreath was awarded.

" 'They're only common people, after all!' thought the Matches.

"Now the Tea Urn was to sing; but she said she had taken cold, and could not sing unless she felt boiling within.

She is waiting still.

[See Page 63]

But that was only affectation; she did not want to sing, except when she was in the parlour with the grand people.

"In the window sat an old Quill Pen, with which the maid generally wrote; there was nothing remarkable about this pen, except that it had been dipped too deep into the ink, but she was proud of that. 'If the Tea Urn won't sing,' she said, 'she may leave it alone. Outside hangs a nightingale in a cage, and he can sing. He hasn't had any education, but this evening we'll say nothing about that.'

" 'I think it very wrong,' said the Tea Kettle—he was the kitchen singer, and half-brother to the Tea Urn—'that that rich and foreign bird should be listened to! Is this patriotic? Let the Market Basket decide.'

" 'I am vexed,' said the Market Basket. 'No one can imagine how much I am secretly vexed. Is that a proper way of spending the evening? Would it not be more sensible to put the house in order? Let each one go to his own place, and I would arrange the whole game. That would be quite another thing.'

" 'Yes, let us make a disturbance,' cried they all. Then the door opened, and the maid came in, and they all stood still; not one stirred. But there was not one pot among them who did not know what he could do, and how grand he was. 'Yes, if I had liked,' each one thought, 'it might have been a very merry evening.'

"The servant girl took the Matches and lighted the fire

with them. Mercy! how they sputtered and burst out into flame! 'Now every one can see,' thought they, 'that we are first. How we shine! what a light!'—and they burned out."

"That was a capital story," said the Sultana. "I feel myself quite carried away to the kitchen, to the Matches. Yes, now thou shalt marry our daughter."

"Yes, certainly," said the Sultan, "thou shalt marry our daughter on Monday."

And they called him *thou*, because he was to belong to the family.

The wedding was decided on, and on the evening before it the whole city was illuminated. Biscuits and cakes were thrown among the people, the street boys stood on their toes, called out "Hurrah!" and whistled on their fingers. It was uncommonly splendid.

"Yes, I shall have to give something as a treat," thought the merchant's son. So he bought rockets and crackers, and every imaginable sort of firework, put them all into his trunk, and flew up into the air.

"Crack!" how they went, and how they went off! All the Turks hopped up with such a start that their slippers flew about their ears; such a meteor they had never yet seen. Now they could understand that it must be a Turkish angel who was going to marry the Princess.

As soon as the merchant's son descended again into the forest with his trunk, he thought. "I will go into the town

now, and hear how it all looked." And it was quite natural that he wanted to do so.

What stories people told! Every one whom he asked about it had seen it in a separate way; but one and all thought it fine.

"I saw the Turkish angel himself," said one. "He had eyes like glowing stars, and a beard like foaming water."

"He flew in a fiery mantle," said another; "the most lovely little cherub peeped forth from among the folds."

Yes, they were wonderful things that he heard; and on the following day he was to be married.

Now he went back to the forest to rest himself in his trunk. But what had become of that? A spark from the fireworks had set fire to it, and the trunk was burned to ashes. He could fly no more, and could not get to his bride.

She stood all day on the roof waiting; and most likely she is waiting still. But he wanders through the world telling fairy tales; but they are not so merry as that one he told about the Matches.

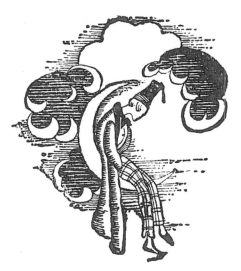

OLE · LUK - OIE

OLE LUK-OIE

HERE'S nobody in the whole world who knows so many stories as Ole Luk-Oie. He can tell capital histories.

Well on in the evening, when the children still sit nicely at table, or upon their stools, Ole Luk-Oie comes. He comes up the stairs quite softly, for he walks in his socks: he opens the door noiselessly, and *whisk!* he squirts sweet milk in the children's eyes, a small, small stream, but enough to prevent them from keeping their eyes open; and thus they cannot see him. He creeps just among them and blows softly upon their necks, and this makes their heads heavy. Yes, but it doesn't hurt them, for Ole Luk-Oie is very fond of the children; he only wants them to be quiet, and *that* they are not until they are taken to bed: they are to be quiet that he may tell them stories.

When the children sleep, Ole Luk-Oie sits down upon their bed. He is well dressed: his coat is of silk, but it is impossible to say of what colour, for it shines red, green, and blue, according as he turns. Under each arm he carries an umbrella: the one with pictures on it he spreads over the good children, and then they dream all night the most glorious stories; but on his other umbrella nothing at all is painted: this he spreads over the naughty children, and these sleep in a dull way, and when they awake in the morning they have not dreamed of anything.

Now we shall hear how Ole Luk-Oie, every evening through one whole week, came to a little boy named Hjalmar, and what he told him. There are seven stories, for there are seven days in the week.

MONDAY

"Listen," said Ole Luk-Oie in the evening, when he had put Hjalmar to bed; "now I'll decorate."

And all the flowers in the flower-pots became great trees, stretching out their long branches under the ceiling of the room and along the walls, so that the whole room looked like a beauteous bower; and all the twigs were covered with flowers, and each flower was more beautiful than a rose, and smelt so sweet that one wanted to eat it—it was sweeter than jam. The fruit gleamed like gold, and there were cakes bursting with raisins. It was incomparably beautiful. But at the same time a terrible wail sounded from the table drawer, where Hjalmar's school-book lay.

"Whatever can that be?" said Ole Luk-Oie; and he went to the table, and opened the drawer. It was the slate which was suffering from convulsions, for a wrong number had got into the sum, so that it was nearly falling in pieces; the slate pencil tugged and jumped at its string, as if it had

68

been a little dog who wanted to help the sum; but he could not. And thus there was a great lamentation in Hjalmar's copy-book; it was quite terrible to hear. On each page the great letters stood in a row, one underneath the other, and each with a little one at its side; that was the copy; and next to these were a few more letters which thought they looked just like the first; and these Hjalmar had written; but they lay down just as if they had tumbled over the pencil lines on which they were to stand.

"See, this is how you should hold yourself," said the Copy. "Look, sloping in this way, with a powerful swing!"

"Oh, we should be very glad to do that," replied Hjalmar's Letters, "but we cannot; we are too weakly."

"Then you must take medicine," said Ole Luk-Oie.

"Oh, no," cried they; and they immediately stood up so gracefully that it was beautiful to behold.

"Yes, now we cannot tell any stories," said Ole Luk-Oie; "now I must exercise them. One, two! one, two!" and thus he exercised the Letters; and they stood quite slender, and as beautiful as any copy can be. But when Ole Luk-Oie went away, and Hjalmar looked at them next morning they were as weak and miserable as ever.

TUESDAY

As soon as Hjalmar was in bed, Ole Luk-Oie touched all the furniture in the room with his little magic squirt,

and they immediately began to converse together, and each one spoke of itself, with the exception of the spittoon, which stood silent, and was vexed that they should be so vain as to speak only of themselves, and think only of themselves, without any regard for him who stood so modestly in the corner for every one's use.

Over the chest of drawers hung a great picture in a gilt frame—it was a landscape. One saw therein large old trees, flowers in the grass, and a large lake with a river which flowed round about a forest, past many castles, and far out into the wide ocean.

Ole Luk-Oie touched the painting with his magic squirt, and the birds in it began to sing, the branches of the trees stirred, and the clouds began to move across it; one could see their shadows glide over the landscape.

Now Ole Luk-Oie lifted little Hjalmar up to the frame, and put the boy's feet into the picture, just in the high grass; and there he stood; and the sun shone upon him through the branches of the trees. He ran to the water, and seated himself in a little boat which lay there; it was painted red and white, the sails gleamed like silver, and six swans, each with a gold circlet round its neck and a bright blue star on its forehead, drew the boat past the great wood, where the trees told of robbers and witches, and the flowers told of the graceful little elves, and of what the butterflies had told them.

Gorgeous fishes, with scales like silver and gold, swam after their boat; sometimes they gave a spring, so that it splashed in the water; and birds, blue and red, little and great, flew after them in two long rows; the gnats danced, and the cockchafers said, "Boom! boom!" They all wanted to follow Hjalmar, and each one had a story to tell.

That *was* a pleasure voyage. Sometimes the forest was thick and dark, sometimes like a glorious garden full of sunlight and flowers; and there were great palaces of glass and of marble; on the balconies stood Princesses, and these were all little girls whom Hjalmar knew well—he had already played with them. Each one stretched forth her hand, and held out the prettiest sugar heart which ever a cake-woman could sell; and Hjalmar took hold of each sugar heart as he passed by, and the Princess held fast, so that each of them got a piece—she the smaller share, and Hjalmar the larger. At each palace little Princes stood sentry. They shouldered golden swords, and caused raisins and tin soldiers to shower down: one could see that they were real Princes. Sometimes Hjalmar sailed through forests, sometimes through great halls or through the midst of a town. He also came to the town where his nurse lived, who had carried him in her arms when he was quite a little boy, and who had always been so kind to him; and she nodded and beckoned, and sang the pretty verse she had made herself and had sent to Hjalmar.

71

OLE LUK-OIE

> I've loved thee, and kissed thee, Hjalmar, dear boy;
> I've watched thee waking and sleeping;
> May the good Lord guard thee in sorrow, in joy,
> And have thee in His keeping

And all the birds sang too, the flowers danced on their stalks, and the old trees nodded, just as if Ole Luk-Oie had been telling stories to *them*.

WEDNESDAY

How the rain was streaming down without! Hjalmar could hear it in his sleep; and when Ole Luk-Oie opened a window, the water stood right up to the window-sill: there was quite a lake outside, and a noble ship lay close by the house.

"If thou wilt sail with me, little Hjalmar," said Ole Luk-Oie, "thou canst voyage to-night to foreign climes, and be back again to-morrow."

And Hjalmar suddenly stood in his Sunday clothes upon the glorious ship, and immediately the weather became fine, and they sailed through the streets, and steered round by the church; and now everything was one great wild ocean. They sailed on until land was no longer to be seen, and they saw a number of storks, who also came from their home, and were travelling towards the hot countries: these storks flew in a row, one behind the other, and they had already flown far—far! One of them was so weary that his wings

That was a pleasure voyage. Sometimes the forest was thick and dark, sometimes like a glorious garden full of sunlight and flowers.

[See Page 71]

would scarcely carry him farther: he was the very last in the row, and soon remained a great way behind the rest; at last he sank, with outspread wings, deeper and deeper; he gave a few more strokes with his pinions, but it was of no use; now he touched the rigging of the ship with his feet, then he glided down from the sail, and—bump!—he stood upon the deck.

Now the cabin boy took him and put him into the hen-coop with the Fowls, Ducks, and Turkeys; the poor Stork stood among them quite embarrassed.

"Just look at the fellow!" said all the Fowls.

And the Turkey-cock swelled himself up as much as ever he could, and asked the Stork who he was; and the Ducks walked backwards and quacked to each other, "Quackery! quackery!"

And the Stork told them of hot Africa, of the pyramids, and of the ostrich, which runs like a wild horse through the desert; but the Ducks did not understand what he said, and they said to one another,

"We're all of the same opinion, namely, that he's stupid."

"Yes, certainly he's stupid," said the Turkey-cock; and he gobbled.

Then the Stork was quite silent, and thought of his Africa.

"Those are wonderful thin legs of yours," said the Turkey-cock. "Pray, how much do they cost a yard?"

"Quack! quack! quack!" grinned all the Ducks; but the Stork pretended not to hear it at all.

"You may just as well laugh too," said the Turkey-cock to him, "for that was very wittily said. Or was it, perhaps, too high for you? Yes, yes, he isn't very penetrating. Let us continue to be interesting among ourselves."

And the Hens clucked, and the Ducks quacked, "Gick! gack! gick! gack!" It was terrible how they made fun among themselves.

But Hjalmar went to the hencoop, opened the back door, and called to the Stork; and the Stork hopped out to him on to the deck. Now he had rested, and it seemed as if he nodded at Hjalmar, to thank him. Then he spread his wings, and flew away to the warm countries; but the Fowls clucked, and the Ducks quacked, and the Turkey-cock became fiery red in the face.

"To-morrow we shall make soup of you," said Hjalmar; and so saying he awoke, and was lying in his little bed. It was a wonderful journey that Ole Luk-Oie had caused him to take that night.

THURSDAY

"I tell you what," said Ole Luk-Oie, "you must not be frightened. Here you shall see a little mouse," and he held out his hand with the pretty little creature in it. "It has

come to invite you to a wedding. There are two little mice here who are going to enter into the marriage state to-night. They live under the floor of your mother's store-closet: that is said to be a charming dwelling-place!"

"But how can I get through the little mouse-hole in the floor?" asked Hjalmar.

"Let me manage that," said Ole Luk-Oie. "I will make you small."

And he touched Hjalmar with his magic squirt, and the boy began to shrink and shrink, until he was not so long as a finger.

"Now you may borrow the uniform of a tin soldier: I think it would fit you, and it looks well to wear a uniform when one is in society."

"Yes, certainly," said Hjalmar.

And in a moment he was dressed like the smartest of tin soldiers.

"Will you not be kind enough to take a seat in your mamma's thimble?" asked the Mouse. "Then I shall have the honour of drawing you."

"Will the young lady really take so much trouble?" cried Hjalmar.

And thus they drove to the mouse's wedding. First they came into a long passage beneath the boards, which was only just so high that they could drive through it in the thimble; and the whole passage was lit up with rotten wood.

"Is there not a delicious smell here?" observed the Mouse. "The entire road has been greased with bacon rinds, and there can be nothing more exquisite."

Now they came into the festive hall. On the right hand stood all the little lady mice; and they whispered and giggled as if they were making fun of each other; on the left stood all the gentlemen mice, stroking their whiskers with their fore paws; and in the centre of the hall the bridegroom and bride might be seen standing in a hollow cheese rind, and kissing each other terribly before all the guests; for of course they were engaged, and were just about to be married.

More and more strangers kept flocking in. One mouse was nearly treading another to death; and the happy couple had stationed themselves just in the doorway, so that one could neither come in or go out. Like the passage the room had been greased with bacon rinds, and that was the entire banquet; but for the dessert a pea was produced, in which a mouse belonging to the family had bitten the name of the betrothed pair—that is to say, the first letter of the name: that was something quite out of the common way.

All the mice said it was a beautiful wedding, and that the entertainment had been very agreeable. And then Hjalmar drove home again: he had really been in grand company; but he had been obliged to shrink in, to make himself little, and to put on a tin soldier's uniform.

FRIDAY

"It is wonderful how many grown-up people there are who would be glad to have me!" said Ole Luk-Oie; "especially those who have done something wrong. 'Good little Ole,' they say to me, 'we cannot close our eyes, and so we lie all night and see our evil deeds, which sit on the bedstead like ugly little goblins, and throw hot water over us; will you not come and drive them away, so that we may have a good sleep?'—and then they sigh deeply—'we would really be glad to pay for it. Good night, Ole; the money lies on the window-sill.' But I do nothing for money," says Ole Luk-Oie.

"What shall we do this evening?" asked Hjalmar.

"I don't know if you care to go to another wedding to-night. It is of a different kind from that of yesterday. Your sister's great doll, that looks like a man, and is called Hermann, is going to marry the doll Bertha. Moreover it is the doll's birthday, and, therefore, they will receive very many presents."

"Yes, I know that," replied Hjalmar. "Whenever the dolls want new clothes my sister lets them either keep their birthday or celebrate a wedding; that has certainly happened a hundred times already."

"Yes, but to-night is the hundred and first wedding; and when number one hundred and one is past, it is all over; and that is why it will be so splendid. Only look!"

OLE LUK-OIE

And Hjalmar looked at the table. There stood the little cardboard house with the windows illuminated, and in front of it all the tin soldiers were presenting arms. The bride and bridegroom sat quite thoughtful, and with good reason, on the floor, leaning against a leg of the table. And Ole Luk-Oie, dressed up in the grandmother's black gown, married them to each other. When the ceremony was over, all the pieces of furniture struck up the following beautiful song, which the pencil had written for them. It was sung to the melody of the soldier's tattoo.

> Let the song swell like the rushing wind,
> In honour of those who this day are joined,
> Although they stand here so stiff and blind,
> . Because they are both of a leathery kind.
> Hurrah! hurrah! though they're deaf and blind,
> Let the song swell like the rushing wind.

And now they received presents—but they had declined to accept provisions of any kind, for they intended to live on love.

"Shall we now go into a summer lodging, or start on a journey?" asked the bridegroom.

And the Swallow, who was a great traveller, and the old yard Hen, who had brought up five broods of chickens, were consulted on the subject. And the Swallow told of the beautiful warm climes, where the grapes hung in ripe heavy clusters, where the air is mild, and the mountains glow with colours unknown here.

"But they have not our green colewort there!" objected the Hen. "I was in the country, with my children one summer. There was a sand pit, in which we could walk about and scratch; and we had the *entrée* to a garden where green colewort grew: Oh, how green it was! I cannot imagine anything more beautiful."

"But one cole-plant looks just like another," said the Swallow; "and the weather here is often so bad."

"One is accustomed to that," said the Hen.

"But it is so cold here, it freezes."

"That is good for the coleworts!" said the Hen. "Besides, it can also be warm. Did we not, four years ago, have a summer which lasted five weeks? it was so hot here that one could scarcely breathe; and then we have not all the poisonous animals that infest these warm countries of yours, and we are free from robbers. He is a villain who does not consider our country the most beautiful—he certainly does not deserve to be here!" And then the Hen wept, and went on: "I have also travelled. I rode in a coop above fifty miles; and there is no pleasure at all in travelling!"

"Yes, the hen is a sensible woman!" said the doll Bertha. "I don't think anything either of travelling among mountains, for you only have to go up, and then down again. No, we will go into the sand pit beyond the gate, and walk about in the colewort-patch."

And so it was settled.

81

OLE LUK-OIE

SATURDAY

"Am I to hear some stories now?" asked little Hjalmar, as soon as Ole Luk-Oie had got him into bed.

"This evening we have no time for that," replied Ole; and he spread his fine umbrella over the lad. "Only look at these Chinamen!"

And the whole umbrella looked like a great China dish, with blue trees and pointed bridges with little Chinamen upon them, who stood there nodding their heads.

"We must have the whole world prettily decked out for to-morrow morning," said Ole, "for that is a holiday—it is Sunday. I will go to the church steeples to see that the little church goblins are polishing the bells, that they may sound sweetly. I will go out into the field, and see if the breezes are blowing the dust from the grass and leaves; and, what is the greatest work of all, I will bring down all the stars, to polish them. I take them in my apron; but first each one must be numbered, and the holes in which they are fixed up there must be numbered likewise, so that they may be placed in the same holes again; otherwise they would not sit fast, and we should have too many shooting stars, for one after another would fall down."

"Hark-ye! Do you know, Mr. Luk-Oie," said an old Portrait which hung on the wall where Hjalmar slept, "I am Hjalmar's great-grandfather. I thank you for telling the boy stories; but you must not confuse his ideas. The stars cannot be taken down and polished! The stars are world-orbs, just like our own earth, and that is just the good thing about them."

"I thank you, old great-grandfather," said Ole Luk-Oie, "I thank you! You are the head of the family. You are the ancestral head; but I am older than you! I am an old heathen: the Romans and Greeks called me the Dream God. I have been in the noblest houses, and am admitted there still! I know how to act with great people and with small. Now you may tell your own story!" And Ole Luk-Oie took his umbrella, and went away.

"Well, well! May one not even give an opinion now-a-days?" grumbled the old Portrait. And Hjalmar awoke.

SUNDAY

"Good evening!" said Ole Luk-Oie; and Hjalmar nodded, and ran and turned his great-grandfather's Portrait against the wall, that it might not interrupt them, as it had done yesterday.

"Now you must tell me stories; about the five green peas that lived in one pod, and about the cock's foot that paid court to the hen's foot, and of the darning-needle who gave herself such airs because she thought herself a sewing needle."

"There may be too much of a good thing!" said Ole Luk-Oie. "You know that I prefer showing you something.

OLE LUK-OIE

I will show you my own brother. His name, like mine, is Ole Luk-Oie, but he never comes to any one more than once; and he takes him to whom he comes upon his horse, and tells him stories. He only knows two. One of these is so exceedingly beautiful that no one in the world can imagine it, and the other so horrible and dreadful that it cannot be described."

And then Ole Luk-Oie lifted little Hjalmar up to the window, and said,

"There you will see my brother the other Ole Luk-Oie. They also call him Death! Do you see, he does not look so terrible as they make him in the picture-books, where he is only a skeleton. No, that is silver embroidery that he has on his coat; that is a splendid hussar's uniform; a mantle of black velvet flies behind him over the horse. See how he gallops along!"

And Hjalmar saw how this Ole Luk-Oie rode away, and took young people as well as old upon his horse. Some of them he put before him, and some behind; but he always asked first, "How stands it with the mark-book?" "Well," they all replied. "Yes, let me see it myself," he said. And then each one had to show him the book; and those who had "very well" and "remarkably well" written in their books, were placed in front of his horse, and a lovely story was told to them; while those who had "middling" or "tolerably well," had to sit up behind, and hear a very terrible story indeed. They trembled and wept, and wanted to jump off

the horse, but this they could not do, for they had all, as it were, grown fast to it.

"But Death is a most splendid Ole Luk-Oie," said Hjalmar. "I am not afraid of him!"

"Nor need you be," replied Ole Luk-Oie; "but see that you have a good mark-book!"

"Yes, that is instructive!" muttered the great-grandfather's Picture. "It is of some use after all giving one's opinion." And now he was satisfied.

You see, that is the story of Ole Luk-Oie; and now he may tell you more himself, this evening!

THE · SWINEHERD

THE SWINEHERD

HERE was once a poor Prince, who had a kingdom which was quite small, but still it was large enough that he could marry upon it, and that is what he wanted to do.

Now, it was certainly somewhat bold of him to say to the Emperor's daughter, "Will you have me?" But he did venture it for his name was famous far and wide: there were hundreds of Princesses who would have been glad to say yes; but did *she* say so? Well, we shall see.

On the grave of the Prince's father there grew a rose bush, a very beautiful rose bush. It bloomed only every fifth year, and even then it bore only a single rose, but what a rose that was! It was so sweet that whoever smelt at it forgot all sorrow and trouble. And then he had a nightingale, which could sing as if all possible melodies were collected in its little throat. This rose and this nightingale the Princess was to have, and therefore they were put into great silver cases and sent to her.

THE SWINEHERD

The Emperor caused the presents to be carried before him into the great hall where the Princess was playing at "visiting" with her maids of honour (they did nothing else), and when she saw the great silver cases with the presents in them, she clapped her hands with joy.

"If it were only a little pussy-cat!" said she.

But then came out the splendid rose.

"Oh, how pretty it is made!" said all the court ladies.

"It is more than pretty," said the Emperor. "It is charming."

But the Princess felt it, and then she almost began to cry.

"Fie, papa," she said, "it is not artificial, it is a *natural* rose!"

"Fie," said all the court ladies, "it's a natural one!"

"Let us first see what is in the other case before we get angry," said the Emperor. And then the nightingale came out; it sang so beautifully that they did not at once know what to say against it.

"*Superbe! charmant!*" said the maids of honour, for they all spoke French, the one worse than the other.

"How that bird reminds me of the late Empress's musical snuff-box," said an old cavalier. "Yes, it is the same tone, the same expression."

"Yes," said the Emperor; and then he wept like a little child.

"I really hope it is not a natural bird," said the Princess.

"Yes, it is a natural bird," said they who had brought it.

"Then let the bird fly away," said the Princess; and she would by no means allow the Prince to come.

But the Prince was not at all dismayed. He stained his face brown and black, drew his hat down over his brows, and knocked at the door.

"Good day, Emperor," he said: "could I not be employed here in the castle?"

"Well," replied the Emperor, "but there are so many who want places; but let me see, I want some one who can keep the pigs, for we have many of them."

So the Prince was appointed the Emperor's swineherd. He received a miserable small room down by the pig-sty, and here he was obliged to stay; but all day long he sat and worked, and when it was evening he had finished a neat little pot, with bells all round it, and when the pot boiled these bells rang out prettily and played the old melody—

Oh, my darling Augustine,
All is lost, all is lost.

But the cleverest thing about the whole arrangement was, that by holding one's finger in the steam from the pot, one could at once smell what food was being cooked at every hearth in the town. That was quite a different thing from the rose.

Now the Princess came with all her maids of honour, and when she heard the melody she stood still and looked quite pleased; for she, too, could play "Oh, my darling Augustine." It was the only thing she could play, but then she played it with one finger.

"Why, that is what I play!" she cried. "He must be an educated swineherd! Hark-ye: go down and ask the price of the instrument."

So one of the maids of honour had to go down; but first she put on a pair of pattens.

"What do you want for the pot?" inquired the lady.

"I want ten kisses from the Princess," replied the swineherd.

"Heaven preserve us!" exclaimed the maid of honour.

"Well, I won't sell it for less," said the swineherd.

"Well, what did he say?" asked the Princess.

"I really can't repeat it, it is so shocking," replied the lady.

"Well, you can whisper it in my ear." And the lady whispered it to her.—"He is very rude," declared the Princess: and she went away. But when she had gone a little way, the bells sounded so prettily—

> Oh, my darling Augustine,
> All is lost, all is lost.

"Hark-ye," said the Princess: "ask him if he will take ten kisses from my maids of honour."

"No, thanks," replied the swineherd: "ten kisses from the Princess, or I shall keep mv pot."

"How tiresome that is!" cried the Princess. "But at least you must stand round me, so that nobody sees it."

And the maids of honour stood round her, and spread out their dresses, and then the swineherd received ten kisses, and she received the pot.

Then there was rejoicing! All the evening and all the day long the pot was kept boiling; there was not a kitchen hearth in the whole town of which they did not know what it had cooked, at the shoemaker's as well as the chamberlain's. The ladies danced with pleasure, and clapped their hands.

"We know who will have sweet soup and pancakes for dinner, and who has hasty pudding and cutlets; how interesting that is!"

"Very interesting!" said the head lady-superintendent.

"Yes, but keep counsel, for I'm the Emperor's daughter."

"Yes, certainly," said all.

The swineherd, that is to say, the Prince—but of course they did not know but that he was a real swineherd—let no day pass by without doing something, and so he made a rattle; when any person swung this rattle, he could play all the waltzes, hops, and polkas that have been known since the creation of the world.

"But that is *superbe!*" cried the Princess, as she went past. "I have never heard a finer composition. Hark-ye: go down and ask what the instrument costs; but I give no more kisses."

"He demands a hundred kisses from the Princess," said the maid of honour who had gone down to make the inquiry.

"I think he must be mad!" exclaimed the Princess; and she went away; but when she had gone a little distance she stood still. "One must encourage art," she observed. "I am the Emperor's daughter! Tell him he shall receive ten kisses, like last time, and he may take the rest from my maids of honour."

"Ah, but we don't like to do it!" said the maids of honour.

"That's all nonsense!" retorted the Princess, "and if I can allow myself to be kissed, you can too; remember, I give you board and wages."

And so the maids of honour had to go down to him again.

"A hundred kisses from the Princess," said he, "or each shall keep his own."

"Stand round me," said she then; and all the maids of honour stood round her while he kissed the Princess.

"What is that crowd down by the pig-sty?" asked the Emperor, who had stepped out to the balcony. He rubbed his eyes and put on his spectacles. "Why, those are the maids of honour, at their tricks, yonder; I shall have to go down to them."

And he pulled up his slippers behind, for they were shoes that he had trodden down at heel. Gracious mercy, how he hurried! So soon as he came down in the court-

And then he went into his kingdom and
  shut the door in her face, and put a
  bar on. So now she might stand
  outside and sing—
    Oh, my darling Augustine,
    All is lost, all is lost.

[See Page 97]

yard, he went quite softly, and the maids of honour were too busy counting the kisses, and seeing fair play, to notice the Emperor. Then he stood on tiptoe.

"What's that?" said he, when he saw that there was kissing going on; and he hit them on the head with his slipper, just as the swineherd was taking the eighty-sixth kiss.

"Be off!" said the Emperor, for he was angry.

And the Princess and the swineherd were both expelled from his dominions. So there she stood and cried, the rain streamed down, and the swineherd scolded.

"Oh, miserable wretch that I am!" said the Princess; "if I had only taken the handsome Prince! Oh, how unhappy I am!"

Then the swineherd went behind a tree, washed the stains from his face, threw away the shabby clothes, and stepped forth in his princely attire, so handsome that the Princess was fain to bow before him.

"I have come to this, that I despise you," said he. "You would not have an honest Prince; you did not value the rose and the nightingale, but for a plaything you kissed the swineherd, and now you have your reward."

And then he went into his kingdom and shut the door in her face, and put a bar on. So now she might stand outside and sing—

> Oh, my darling Augustine,
> All is lost, all is lost.

THE · NIGHTINGALE

THE NIGHTINGALE

IN China, you must know, the Emperor is a Chinaman, and all whom he has about him are Chinamen too. It happened a good many years ago, but that's just why it's worth while to hear the story, before it is forgotten. The Emperor's palace was the most splendid in the world; it was made entirely of porcelain, very costly, but so delicate and brittle that one had to take care how one touched it. In the garden were to be seen the most wonderful flowers, and to the costliest of them silver bells were tied, which sounded, so that nobody should pass by without noticing the flowers. Yes, everything in the Emperor's garden was admirably arranged. And it extended so far that the gardener himself did not know where the end was. If a man went on and on, he came into a glorious forest with high trees and deep lakes. The wood extended straight down to the sea, which was blue and deep; great ships could sail in beneath the branches of the trees; and in the trees lived a Nightingale, which sang so splendidly that even the poor fisherman, who had many other things to do, stopped still and listened, when he had gone out at night to take up his nets, and heard the Nightingale.

"How beautiful that is!" he said; but he was obliged to attend to his business, and thus forgot the bird. But when in the next night the bird sang again, and the fisherman heard it, he exclaimed again, "how beautiful that is!"

From all the countries of the world travellers came to the city of the Emperor, and admired it, and the palace and the garden, but when they heard the Nightingale, they said, "That is the best of all!"

And the travellers told of it when they came home; and the learned men wrote many books about the town, the palace and the garden. But they did not forget the Nightingale; that was placed highest of all; and those who were poets wrote most magnificent poems about the Nightingale in the wood by the deep lake.

The books went through all the world, and a few of them once came to the Emperor. He sat in his golden chair, and read, and read: every moment he nodded his head, for it pleased him to peruse the masterly descriptions of the city, the palace, and the garden. "But the Nightingale is the best of all," it stood written there.

"What's that?" exclaimed the Emperor. "I don't know the Nightingale at all! Is there such a bird in my empire, and even in my garden? I've never heard of that. To

think that I should have to learn such a thing for the first time from books!"

And hereupon he called his cavalier. This cavalier was so grand that if any one lower in rank than himself dared to speak to him, or to ask him any question, he answered nothing but "P!"—and that meant nothing.

"There is said to be a wonderful bird here called a Nightingale!" said the Emperor. "They say it is the best thing in all my great empire. Why have I never heard anything about it!"

"I have never heard him named," replied the cavalier. "He has never been introduced at court."

"I command that he shall appear this evening, and sing before me," said the Emperor. "All the world knows what I possess, and I do not know it myself!"

"I have never heard him mentioned," said the cavalier. "I will seek for him. I will find him."

But where was he to be found? The cavalier ran up and down all the staircases, through halls and passages, but no one among all those whom he met had heard talk of the Nightingale. And the cavalier ran back to the Emperor, and said that it must be a fable invented by the writers of books.

"Your Imperial Majesty cannot believe how much is written that is fiction, besides something that they call the black art."

"But the book in which I read this," said the Emperor,

"was sent to me by the high and mighty Emperor of Japan, and therefore it cannot be a falsehood. I *will* hear the Nightingale! It must be here this evening! It has my imperial favour; and if it does not come, all the court shall be trampled upon after the court has supped!"

"Tsing-pe!" said the cavalier; and again he ran up and down all the staircases, and through all the halls and corridors; and half the court ran with him, for the courtiers did not like being trampled upon.

Then there was a great inquiry after the wonderful Nightingale, which all the world knew excepting the people at court.

At last they met with a poor little girl in the kitchen, who said,

"The Nightingale? I know it well; yes, it can sing gloriously. Every evening I get leave to carry my poor sick mother the scraps from the table. She lives down by the strand, and when I get back and am tired, and rest in the wood, then I hear the Nightingale sing. And then the water comes into my eyes, and it is just as if my mother kissed me!"

"Little girl," said the cavalier, "I will get you a place in the kitchen, with permission to see the Emperor dine, if you will lead us to the Nightingale, for it is announced for this evening."

So they all went out into the wood where the Nightingale was accustomed to sing; half the court went forth.

When they were in the midst of their journey a cow began to low.

"Oh!" cried the court page, "now we have it! That shows a wonderful power in so small a creature! I have certainly heard it before."

"No, those are cows lowing!" said the little kitchen-girl. "We are a long way from the place yet."

Now the frogs began to croak in the marsh.

"Glorious!" said the Chinese court preacher. "Now I hear it—it sounds just like little church bells."

"No, those are frogs!" said the little kitchen-maid. "But now I think we shall soon hear it."

And then the Nightingale began to sing.

"That is it!" exclaimed the little girl. "Listen, listen! and yonder it sits."

And she pointed to a little grey bird up in the boughs.

"Is it possible?" cried the cavalier. "I should never have thought it looked like that! How plain it looks! It must certainly have lost its colour at seeing such grand people around."

"Little Nightingale!" called the little kitchen-maid, quite loudly, "our gracious Emperor wishes you to sing before him."

"With the greatest pleasure!" replied the Nightingale, and began to sing most delightfully.

"It sounds just like glass bells!" said the cavalier. "And look at its little throat, how it's working! It's wonderful that we should never have heard it before. That bird will be a great success at court."

"Shall I sing once more before the Emperor?" asked the Nightingale, for it thought the Emperor was present.

"My excellent little Nightingale," said the cavalier, "I have great pleasure in inviting you to a court festival this evening, when you shall charm his Imperial Majesty with your beautiful singing."

"My song sounds best in the green wood!" replied the Nightingale; still it came willingly when it heard what the Emperor wished.

The palace was festively adorned. The walls and the flooring, which were of porcelain, gleamed in the rays of thousands of golden lamps. The most glorious flowers, which could ring clearly, had been placed in the passages. There was a running to and fro, and a thorough draught, and all the bells rang so loudly that one could not hear oneself speak.

In the midst of the great hall, where the Emperor sat, a golden perch had been placed, on which the Nightingale was to sit. The whole court was there, and the little kitchen-maid had got leave to stand behind the door, as she had now received the title of a real court cook. All were in full dress, and all looked at the little grey bird, to which the Emperor nodded.

And the Nightingale sang so gloriously that the tears came into the Emperor's eyes, and the tears ran down over

And when I get back and am tired, and
rest in the wood, then I hear the
Nightingale sing.

[See Page 104]

his cheeks; and then the Nightingale sang still more sweetly, so that its song went straight to the heart. The Emperor was so much pleased that he said the Nightingale should have his golden slipper to wear round its neck. But the Nightingale declined this with thanks, saying it had already received a sufficient reward.

"I have seen tears in the Emperor's eyes—that is the real treasure to me. An Emperor's tears have a peculiar power. I am rewarded enough!" And then it sang again with a sweet glorious voice.

"That's the most amiable coquetry I ever saw!" said the ladies who stood round about, and then they took water in their mouths to gurgle when any one spoke to them. They thought they should be nightingales too. And the lackeys and chambermaids reported that they were satisfied too; and that was saying a good deal, for they are the most difficult to please. In short, the Nightingale achieved a real success.

It was now to remain at court, to have its own cage, with liberty to go out twice every day and once at night. Twelve servants were appointed when the Nightingale went out, each of whom had a silken string fastened to the bird's leg, and which they held very tight. There was really no pleasure in an excursion of that kind.

The whole city spoke of the wonderful bird, and when two people met, one said nothing but "Nightin," and the other "gale"; and then they sighed, and understood one

another. Eleven pedlars' children were named after the bird, but not one of them could sing a note.

One day the Emperor received a large parcel, on which was written "The Nightingale."

"There we have a new book about this celebrated bird," said the Emperor.

But it was not a book, but a little work of art, contained in a box, an artificial nightingale, which was to sing like the natural one, and was brilliantly ornamented with diamonds, rubies, and sapphires. So soon as the artificial bird was wound up, he could sing one of the pieces that the real one sang, and then his tail moved up and down, and shone with silver and gold. Round his neck hung a little ribbon, and on that was written, "The Emperor of Japan's nightingale is poor compared to that of the Emperor of China."

"That is capital!" said they all, and he who had brought the artificial bird immediately received the title, Imperial Head-Nightingale-Bringer.

"Now they must sing together; what a duet that will be!"

And so they had to sing together; but it did not sound very well, for the real Nightingale sang in its own way, and the artificial bird sang waltzes.

"That's not his fault," said the playmaster; "he's quite perfect, and very much in my style."

Now the artificial bird was to sing alone. He had just as much success as the real one, and then it was much handsomer to look at—it shone like bracelets and breast-pins.

Three and thirty times over did it sing the same piece, and yet was not tired. The people would gladly have heard it again, but the Emperor said that the living Nightingale ought to sing something now. But where was it? No one had noticed that it had flown away out of the open window, back to the green wood.

"But what in all the world is this?" said the Emperor. And all the courtiers abused the Nightingale, and declared that it was a very ungrateful creature.

"We have the best bird, after all," said they.

And so the artificial bird had to sing again, and that was the thirty-fourth time that they listened to the same piece. For all that they did not know it quite by heart, for it was so very difficult. And the playmaster praised the bird particularly; yes, he declared that it was better than a nightingale, not only with regard to its plumage and the many beautiful diamonds, but inside as well.

"For you see, ladies and gentlemen, and above all, your Imperial Majesty, with a real nightingale one can never calculate what is coming, but in this artificial bird everything is settled. One can explain it; one can open it and make people understand where the waltzes come from, how they go, and how one follows up another."

"Those are quite our own ideas," they all said.

And the speaker received permission to show the bird

to the people on the next Sunday. The people were to hear it sing too, the Emperor commanded; and they did hear it, and were as much pleased as if they had all got tipsy upon tea, for that's quite the Chinese fashion; and they all said, "Oh!" and held up their forefingers and nodded. But the poor fisherman who had heard the real Nightingale, said,

"It sounds pretty enough, and the melodies resemble each other, but there's something wanting, though I know not what!"

The real Nightingale was banished from the country and empire. The artificial bird had its place on a silken cushion close to the Emperor's bed; all the presents it had received, gold and precious stones, were ranged about it; in title it had advanced to be the High Imperial Night-Singer, and in rank to number one on the left hand; for the Emperor considered that side the most important on which the heart is placed, and even in an Emperor the heart is on the left side; and the playmaster wrote a work of five-and-twenty volumes about the artificial bird; it was very learned and very long, full of the most difficult Chinese words; but yet all the people declared that they had read it and understood it, for fear of being considered stupid, and having their bodies trampled on.

So a whole year went by. The Emperor, the court, and all the other Chinese knew every little twitter in the artificial bird's song by heart. But just for that reason it pleased them best—they could sing with it themselves, and they did

so. The street boys sang, "Tsi-tsi-tsi-glug-glug!" and the Emperor himself sang it too. Yes, that was certainly famous.

But one evening, when the artificial bird was singing its best, and the Emperor lay in bed listening to it, something inside the bird said, "Whizz!" Something cracked. "Whir-r-r!" All the wheels ran round, and then the music stopped.

The Emperor immediately sprang out of bed, and caused his body physician to be called; but what could *he* do? Then they sent for a watchmaker, and after a good deal of talking and investigation, the bird was put into something like order; but the watchmaker said that the bird must be carefully treated, for the barrels were worn, and it would be impossible to put new ones in in such a manner that the music would go. There was a great lamentation; only once in a year was it permitted to let the bird sing, and that was almost too much. But then the playmaster made a little speech, full of hard words, and said this was just as good as before—and so of course it was as good as before.

Now five years had gone by, and a real grief came upon the whole nation. The Chinese were really fond of their Emperor, and now he was ill, and could not, it was said, live much longer. Already a new Emperor had been chosen, and the people stood out in the street and asked the cavalier how their old Emperor did.

"P!" said he, and shook his head.

Cold and pale lay the Emperor in his great gorgeous bed; the whole court thought him dead, and each one ran to pay homage to the new ruler. The chamberlains ran out to talk it over, and the ladies'-maids had a great coffee party. All about, in all the halls and passages, cloth had been laid down so that no footstep could be heard, and therefore it was quiet there, quite quiet. But the Emperor was not dead yet; stiff and pale he lay on the gorgeous bed with the long velvet curtains and the heavy gold tassels; high up, a window stood open, and the moon shone in upon the Emperor and the artificial bird.

The poor Emperor could scarcely breathe; it was just as if something lay upon his chest: he opened his eyes, and then he saw that it was Death who sat upon his chest, and had put on his golden crown, and held in one hand the Emperor's sword, and in the other his beautiful banner. And all around, from among the folds of the splendid velvet curtains, strange heads peered forth; a few very ugly, the rest quite lovely and mild. These were all the Empror's bad and good deeds, that looked upon him now that Death sat upon his heart.

"Do you remember this?" whispered one after the other, "Do you remember that?" and then they told him so much that the perspiration ran from his forehead.

"I did not know that!" said the Emperor. "Music!

music! the great Chinese drum!" he cried, "so that I need not hear all they say!"

And they continued speaking, and Death nodded like a Chinaman to all they said.

"Music! music!" cried the Emperor. "You little precious golden bird, sing, sing! I have given you gold and costly presents; I have even hung my golden slipper around your neck—sing now, sing!"

But the bird stood still; no one was there to wind him up, and he could not sing without that; but Death continued to stare at the Emperor with his great hollow eyes, and it was quiet, fearfully quiet.

Then there sounded from the window, suddenly, the most lovely song. It was the little live Nightingale, that sat outside on a spray. It had heard of the Emperor's sad plight, and had come to sing to him of comfort and hope. And as it sang the spectres grew paler and paler; the blood ran quicker and more quickly through the Emperor's weak limbs; and even Death listened, and said,

"Go on, little Nightingale, go on!"

"But will you give me that splendid golden sword? Will you give me that rich banner? Will you give me the Emperor's Crown?"

And Death gave up each of these treasures for a song. And the Nightingale sang on and on; and it sang of the quiet churchyard where the white roses grow, where the elder-blossom smells sweet, and where the fresh grass is moistened by the tears of survivors. Then Death felt a longing to see his garden, and floated out at the window in the form of a cold white mist.

"Thanks! thanks!" said the Emperor. "You heavenly little bird! I know you well. I banished you from my country and empire, and yet you have charmed away the evil faces from my couch, and banished Death from my heart! How can I reward you?"

"You have rewarded me!" replied the Nightingale. "I have drawn tears from your eyes, when I sang the first time—I shall never forget that. Those are the jewels that rejoice a singer's heart. But now sleep and grow fresh and strong again. I will sing you something."

And it sang, and the Emperor fell into a sweet slumber. Ah! how mild and refreshing that sleep was! The sun shone upon him through the windows, when he awoke refreshed and restored: not one of his servants had yet returned, for they all thought he was dead; only the Nightingale still sat beside him and sang.

"You must always stay with me," said the Emperor. "You shall sing as you please; and I'll break the artificial bird into a thousand pieces."

"Not so," replied the Nightingale. "It did well as long as it could; keep it as you have done till now. I cannot build my nest in the palace to dwell in it, but let me come when I feel the wish; then I will sit in the evening on the spray yonder by the window, and sing you something, so that you may be glad and thoughtful at once. I will sing of those who are happy and of those who suffer. I will sing of the good and the evil that remains hidden round about you. The little singing bird flies far around, to the poor fisherman, to the peasant's roof, to every one who dwells far away from you and from your court. I love your heart more than your crown, and yet the crown has an air of sanctity about it. I will come and sing to you— but one thing you must promise me."

"Everything!" said the Emperor; and he stood there in his imperial robes, which he had put on himself, and pressed the sword which was heavy with gold to his heart.

"One thing I beg of you: tell no one that you have a little bird who tells you everything. Then it will go all the better."

And the Nightingale flew away.

The servants came in to look at their dead Emperor, and—yes, there they stood, and the Emperor said "Good morning!"

THE · SNOW · QUEEN

THE SNOW QUEEN

In Seven Stories

FIRST STORY

WHICH TREATS OF THE MIRROR AND FRAGMENTS

OOK you, now we're going to begin. When we are at the end of the story we shall know more than we do now, for he was a bad goblin. He was one of the very worst, for he was the devil himself. One day he was in very high spirits, for he had made a mirror which had this peculiarity, that everything good and beautiful that was reflected in it shrank together into almost nothing, but that whatever was worthless and looked ugly became prominent and looked worse than ever. The most lovely landscapes seen in this mirror looked like boiled spinach, and the best people became hideous, or stood on their heads and had no stomachs; their faces were so distorted as to be unrecognisable, and a single freckle was shown spread out over nose and mouth. That was very amusing, the devil said. When a good pious thought passed through any person's mind, there came a grin in the mirror, so that the devil chuckled at his artistic invention. Those who went to the goblin school—for he kept a goblin school—declared everywhere that a wonder had been wrought. For now, they asserted, one could see, for the first time, how the world and the people in it really looked. They ran about with the mirror, and at last there was not a single country or person that had not been distorted in it. Now they wanted to fly up to heaven, to sneer and scoff at the angels themselves. The higher they flew with the mirror, the more it grinned; they could scarcely hold it fast. They flew higher and higher, and then the mirror trembled so terribly amid its grinning that it fell down out of their hands to the earth, where it was shattered into a hundred million million and more fragments. And now this mirror occasioned much more unhappiness than before; for some of the fragments were scarcely so large as a barley-corn, and these flew about in the world and whenever they flew in any one's eye they stuck there, and those people saw everything wrongly, or had only eyes for the bad side of a thing, for every little fragment of the mirror had retained the same power which the whole glass possessed. A few persons even got a fragment of the mirror into their hearts, and that was terrible indeed, for such a heart became a block of ice. A few fragments of the mirror were so large that they were used as window-panes, but it was a bad thing to look at one's friends through these panes; other pieces were made into spectacles, and then it went badly

A few persons even got a fragment of the
mirror into their hearts, and that
was terrible indeed, for such a heart
became a block of ice.

[See Page 122]

when people put on these spectacles to see rightly and to be just; and the demon laughed till his paunch shook, for it tickled him so. But without, some little fragments of glass still floated about in the air—and now we shall hear.

SECOND STORY

A LITTLE BOY AND A LITTLE GIRL

In the great town, where there are many houses and so many people that there is not room enough for every one to have a little garden, and where, consequently, most persons are compelled to be content with some flowers in flower-pots, were two poor children who possessed a garden somewhat larger than a flower-pot. They were not brother and sister, but they loved each other quite as much as if they had been. Their parents lived just opposite each other in two garrets, there where the roof on one neighbour's house joined that of another; and where the water-pipe ran between the two houses was a little window; one had only to step across the pipe to get from one window to the other.

The parents of each child had a great box, in which grew kitchen herbs that they used, and a little rose bush; there was one in each box, and they grew famously. Now it occurred to the parents to place the boxes across the pipe, so that they reached from one window to another, and looked quite like two embankments of flowers. Pea plants hung down over the boxes, and the rose bushes shot forth long

twigs, which clustered round the windows and bent down towards each other: it was almost like a triumphal arch of flowers and leaves. As the boxes were very high, and the children knew that they might not creep upon them, they often obtained permission to step out upon the roof behind the boxes, and to sit upon their stools under the roses, and there they could play capitally.

In the winter there was an end of this amusement. The windows were sometimes quite frozen all over. But then they warmed copper farthings on the stove, and held the warm coins against the frozen pane; and this made a capital peep-hole so round, so round! and behind it gleamed a pretty mild eye at each window; and these eyes belonged to the little boy and the little girl. His name was Kay and the little girl's was Gerda.

In the summer they could get to one another at one bound; but in the winter they had to go down and up the long staircase, while the snow was pelting without.

"Those are the white bees swarming," said the old grandmother.

"Have they a Queen-bee?" asked the little boy. For he knew that there is one among the real bees.

"Yes, they have one," replied grandmamma. "She always flies where they swarm thickest. She is the largest of them all, and never remains quite upon the earth; she flies up again into the black cloud. Many a midnight she is flying through the streets of the town, and looks in at the windows, and then they freeze in such a strange way, and look like flowers."

"Yes, I've seen that!" cried both the children; and now they knew that it was true.

"Can the Snow Queen come in here?" asked the little girl.

"Only let her come," cried the boy; "I'll set her upon the warm stove, and then she'll melt."

But grandmother smoothed his hair, and told some other tales.

In the evening, when little Kay was at home and half undressed, he clambered upon the chair by the window, and looked through the little hole. A few flakes of snow were falling outside, and one of them, the largest of them all, remained lying on the edge of one of the flower-boxes. The snowflake grew larger and larger, and at last became a maiden clothed in finest white gauze, made out of millions of starry flakes. She was beautiful and delicate, but of ice—of shining, glittering ice. Yet she was alive; her eyes flashed like two clear stars, but there was no peace or rest in them. She nodded towards the window, and beckoned with her hand. The little boy was frightened, and sprang down from the chair; then it seemed as if a great bird flew by outside, in front of the window.

Next day there was a clear frost, then there was a thaw, and then the spring came; the sun shone, the green sprouted forth, the swallows built nests, the windows were opened,

and the little children again sat in their garden high up in the roof over all the floors.

How splendidly the roses bloomed this summer! The little girl had learned a psalm, in which mention was made of roses; and in speaking of roses, she thought of her own; and she sang it to the little boy, and he sang too,—

> The roses in the valleys grow
> Where we the infant Christ shall know.

And the little ones held each other by the hand, kissed the roses, looked at God's bright sunshine, and spoke to it, as if the Christchild were there. What splendid summer days those were! How beautiful it was without, among the fresh rose bushes, which seemed as if they would never leave off blooming!

Kay and Gerda sat and looked at the picture-book of beasts and birds. Then it was, while the clock was just striking five on the church tower, that Kay said,

"Oh! something struck my heart and pricked me in the eye."

The little girl fell upon his neck; he blinked his eyes. No, there was nothing at all to be seen.

"I think it is gone," said he; but it was not gone. It was just one of those glass fragments which sprang from the mirror—the magic mirror that we remember well, the ugly glass that made everything great and good which was mirrored in it to seem small and mean, but in which the

mean and wicked things were brought out in relief, and every fault was noticeable at once. Poor little Kay had also received a splinter just in his heart, and that will now soon become like a lump of ice. It did not hurt him now, but the splinter was still there.

"Why do you cry?" he asked. "You look ugly like that. There's nothing the matter with me. Oh, fie!" he suddenly exclaimed, "that rose is worm-eaten, and this one is quite crooked. After all, they're ugly roses. They're like the box in which they stand."

And then he kicked the box with his foot, and tore both the roses off.

"Kay, what are you about?" cried the little girl.

And when he noticed her fright he tore off another rose, and then sprang in at his own window, away from pretty little Gerda.

When she afterwards came with her picture-book, he said it was only fit for babies in arms; and when grandmother told stories he always came in with a *but;* and when he could manage it he would get behind her, put on a pair of spectacles, and talk just as she did; he could do that very cleverly, and the people laughed at him. Soon he could mimic the speech and the gait of everybody in the street. Everything that was peculiar or ugly about them Kay could imitate; and people said, "That boy must certainly have a remarkable head." But it was the glass he had got in his eye, the glass that stuck deep in his heart; so it happened that he even teased little Gerda, who loved him with all her heart.

His games now became quite different from what they were before; they became quite sensible. One winter's day when it snowed he came out with a great burning glass, held up the blue tail of his coat, and let the snowflakes fall into it.

"Now look at the glass, Gerda," said he.

And every flake of snow was magnified, and looked like a splendid flower, or a star with ten points: it was beautiful to behold.

"See how clever that is," said Kay. "That's much more interesting than real flowers; and there is not a single fault in it—they're quite regular until they begin to melt."

Soon after Kay came in thick gloves, and with his sledge upon his back. He called up to Gerda, "I've got leave to go into the great square, where the other boys play," and he was gone.

In the great square the boldest among the boys often tied their sledges to the country people's carts, and thus rode with them a good way. They went capitally. When they were in the midst of their playing there came a great sledge. It was painted quite white, and in it sat somebody wrapped in a rough white fur, and with a white rough cap on his head. The sledge drove twice round the square, and Kay bound his little sledge to it, and so he drove on with it. It went faster and faster, straight into the next

street. The man who drove turned round and nodded in a friendly way to Kay; it was as if they knew one another: each time when Kay wanted to cast loose his little sledge, the stranger nodded again, and then Kay remained where he was, and thus they drove out at the town gate. Then the snow began to fall so rapidly that the boy could not see a hand's breadth before him, but still he drove on. Now he hastily dropped the cord, so as to get loose from the great sledge, but that was no use, for his sledge was fast bound to the other, and they went on like the wind. Then he called out quite loudly, but nobody heard him; and the snow beat down, and the sledge flew onward; every now and then it gave a jump, and they seemed to be flying over hedges and ditches. The boy was quite frightened. He wanted to say his prayers, but could remember nothing but the multiplication table.

The snowflakes became larger and larger; at last they looked like great white fowls. All at once they sprang aside and the great sledge stopped, and the person who had driven it rose up. The fur and the cap were made altogether of ice. It was *a lady*, tall and slender, and brilliantly white: it was the Snow Queen.

"We have driven well!" said she. "But why do you tremble with cold? Creep into my fur."

And she seated him beside her in her own sledge, and wrapped the fur round him, and he felt as if he had sank into a snow-drift.

131

"Are you still cold?" asked she, and she kissed him on the forehead.

Oh, that was colder than ice; it went quite through to his heart, half of which was already a lump of ice: he felt as if he were going to die; but only for a moment; for then he seemed quite well, and he did not notice the cold all about him.

"My sledge! don't forget my sledge."

That was the first thing he thought of; and it was bound fast to one of the white chickens, and this chicken flew behind him with the sledge upon his back. The Snow Queen kissed Kay again, and then he had forgotten little Gerda, his grandmother and all at home.

"Now you shall have no more kisses," said she, "for if you do I should kiss you to death."

Kay looked at her. She was so beautiful, he could not imagine a more sensible or lovely face; she did not appear to him to be made of ice now as before, when she sat at the window and beckoned to him. In his eyes she was perfect; he did not feel at all afraid. He told her that he could do mental arithmetic as far as fractions, that he knew the number of square miles, and the number of inhabitants in the country. And she always smiled and then it seemed to him that what he knew was not enough, and he looked up into the wide sky, and she flew with him high up upon the black cloud, and the storm blew and whistled; it seemed as though the wind sang old songs. They flew over woods and lakes, over sea and land: below them roared the cold wind, the wolves howled, the snow crackled; over them flew the black screaming crows; but above all the moon shone bright and clear, and Kay looked at the long, long winter night; by day he slept at the feet of the Queen.

THIRD STORY

THE FLOWER GARDEN OF THE WOMAN WHO COULD CONJURE

But how did it fare with little Gerda when Kay did not return? What could have become of him? No one knew, no one could give information. The boys only told that they had seen him bind his sledge to another very large one, which had driven along the street and out at the town gate. Nobody knew what had become of him; many tears were shed, and little Gerda especially wept long and bitterly; then they said he was dead—he had been drowned in the river which flowed close by their town. Oh, those were very dark long winter days! But now spring came, with warmer sunshine.

"Kay is dead and gone," said little Gerda.

"I don't believe it," said the Sunshine.

"He is dead and gone," said she to the Swallows.

"We don't believe it," they replied; and at last little Gerda did not believe it herself.

"I will put on my new red shoes," she said one morning,

"those that Kay has never seen; and then I will go down to the river, and ask for him."

It was still very early; she kissed the old grandmother, who was still asleep, put on her red shoes, and went quite alone out of the town gate towards the river.

"Is it true that you have taken away my little playmate from me? I will give you my red shoes if you will give him back to me!"

And it seemed to her as if the waves nodded quite strangely; and then she took her red shoes, that she liked best of anything she possessed, and threw them both into the river; but they fell close to the shore, and the little wavelets carried them back to her, to the land. It seemed as if the river would not take from her the dearest things she possessed because it had not her little Kay; but she thought she had not thrown the shoes far enough out; so she crept into a boat that lay among the reeds; she went to the other end of the boat, and threw the shoes from thence into the water; but the boat was not bound fast, and at the movement she made it glided away from the shore. She noticed it, and hurried to get back, but before she reached the other end the boat was a yard from the bank, and it drifted away faster than before.

Then little Gerda was very much frightened, and began to cry; but no one heard her except the Sparrows, and they could not carry her to land; but they flew along by the shore, and sang, as if to console her, "Here we are! here we are!"

The boat drove on with the stream, and little Gerda sat quite still, with only her stockings on her feet; her little red shoes floated along behind her, but they could not come up to the boat, for that made more way.

It was very pretty on both shores. There were beautiful flowers, old trees, and slopes with sheep and cows; but not *one* person was to be seen.

"Perhaps the river will carry me to Kay," thought Gerda.

And then she became more cheerful, and rose up, and for many hours she watched the charming green banks; then she came to a great cherry orchard, in which stood a little house with remarkable blue and red windows; it had a thatched roof, and without stood two wooden soldiers, who presented arms to those who sailed past.

Gerda called to them, for she thought they were alive, but of course they did not answer. She came quite close to them; the river carried the boat towards the shore.

Gerda called still louder, and then there came out of the house an old, old woman leaning on a crutch: she had on a great sun-hat, painted over with the finest flowers.

"You poor little child!" said the old woman, "how did you manage to come on the great rolling river, and to float thus far out into the world?"

And then the old woman went quite into the water, seized the boat with her crutch-stick, drew it to land, and lifted little Gerda out. And Gerda was glad to be on dry land again, though she felt a little afraid of the strange old woman.

"Come and tell me who you are, and how you came here," said the old lady. And Gerda told her everything; and the old woman shook her head, and said, "Hem! hem!" And when Gerda had told everything, and asked if she had not seen little Kay the woman said that he had not yet come by, but that he probably would soon come. Gerda was not to be sorrowful, but to look at the flowers and taste the cherries, for they were better than any picture-book, for each one of them could tell a story. Then she took Gerda by the hand and led her into the little house, and the old woman locked the door.

The windows were very high, and the panes were red, blue and yellow; the daylight shone in a remarkable way, with different colours. On the table stood the finest cherries, and Gerda ate as many of them as she liked, for she had leave to do so. While she was eating them, the old lady combed her hair with a golden comb and the hair hung in ringlets of pretty yellow round the friendly little face, which looked as blooming as a rose.

"I have long wished for such a dear little girl as you," said the old lady. "Now you shall see how well we shall live with one another."

And as the ancient dame combed her hair, Gerda forgot her adopted brother Kay more and more; for this old woman could conjure. but she was not a wicked witch. She only practised a little magic for her own amusement, and wanted to keep little Gerda. Therefore she went into the garden, stretched out her crutch towards all the rose-bushes, and, beautiful as they were, they all sank into the earth, and one could not tell where they had stood. The old woman was afraid that if the little girl saw roses, she would think of her own, and remember little Kay, and run away.

Now Gerda was led out into the flower-garden. What fragrance was there, and what loveliness! Every conceivable flower was there in full bloom; there were some for every season: no picture-book could be gayer and prettier. Gerda jumped high for joy, and played till the sun went down behind the high cherry-trees; then she was put into a lovely bed with red silk pillows stuffed with blue violets, and she slept there, and dreamed as gloriously as a Queen on her wedding-day.

One day she played again with the flowers in the warm sunshine; and thus many days went by. Gerda knew every flower; but, as many as there were of them, it still seemed to her as if one were wanting, but which one she did not know. One day she sat looking at the old lady's hat with the painted flowers, and the prettiest of them all was a rose. The old lady had forgotten to take it out of her hat when she caused the others to disappear. But so it always is when one does not keep one's wits about one.

"What, are there no roses here?" cried Gerda.

And she went among the beds, and searched and searched,

but there was not one to be found. Then she sat down and wept: her tears fell just upon a spot where a rose-bush lay buried, and when the warm tears moistened the earth, the bush at once sprouted up as blooming as when it had sunk; and Gerda embraced it, and kissed the Roses, and thought of the beautiful roses at home, and also of little Kay.

"Oh, how I have been detained!" said the little girl. "I wanted to seek for little Kay! Do you know where he is?" she asked the Roses. "Do you think he is dead?"

"He is not dead," the Roses answered. "We have been in the ground. All the dead people are there, but Kay is not there."

"Thank you," said little Gerda; and she went to the other flowers, looked into their cups, and asked, "Do you not know where little Kay is?"

But every flower stood in the sun thinking only of her own story or fairy tale: Gerda heard many, many of them; but not one knew anything of Kay.

And what did the Tiger-Lily say?

"Do you hear the drum 'rub-dub'? There are only two notes, always 'rub-dub!' Hear the morning song of the women, hear the call of the priests. The Hindoo widow stands in her long red mantle on the funeral pile; the flames rise up around her and her dead husband; but the Hindoo woman is thinking of the living one here in the circle, of him whose eyes burn hotter than flames whose fiery glances

have burned in her soul more ardently than the flames themselves, which are soon to burn her body to ashes. Can the flame of the heart die in the flame of the funeral pile?"

"I don't understand that at all!" said little Gerda.

"That's my story," said the Lily.

What says the Convolvulus?

"Over the narrow road looms an old knightly castle: thickly the ivy grows over the crumbling red walls, leaf by leaf up to the balcony, and there stands a beautiful girl; she bends over the balustrade and looks down at the road. No rose on its branch is fresher than she; no apple blossom wafted onward by the wind floats more lightly along. How her costly silks rustle! 'Comes he not yet?' "

"Is it Kay whom you mean?" asked little Gerda.

"I'm only speaking of my own story—my dream," replied the Convolvulus.

What said the little Snowdrop?

"Between the trees a long board hangs by ropes; that is a swing. Two pretty little girls, with clothes white as snow and long green silk ribbons on their hats, are sitting upon it, swinging; their brother, who is greater than they, stands in the swing, and has slung his arm round the rope to hold himself, for in one hand he has a little saucer, and in the other a clay pipe; he is blowing bubbles. The swing flies and the bubbles rise with beautiful changing colours; the last still hangs from the pipe-bowl, swaying in the wind. The swing flies on: the little black dog, light as the bubbles, stands up on his hind legs and wants to be taken into the swing; it flies on, and the dog falls, barks and grows angry, for he is teased, and the bubble bursts. A swinging board and a bursting bubble—that is my song."

"It may be very pretty, what you're telling, but you speak it so mournfully, and you don't mention little Kay at all."

What do the Hyacinths say?

"There were three beautiful sisters, transparent and delicate. The dress of one was red, that of the second blue, and that of the third quite white; hand in hand they danced by the calm lake in the bright moonlight. They were not elves, they were human beings. It was so sweet and fragrant there! The girls disappeared in the forest, and the sweet fragrance became stronger: three coffins with the three beautiful maidens lying in them, glided from the wood-thicket across the lake; the glow-worms flew gleaming about them like little hovering lights. Are the dancing girls sleeping, or are they dead? The flower-scent says they are dead and the evening bell tolls their knell."

"You make me quite sorrowful," said little Gerda. "You scent so strongly, I cannot help thinking of the dead maidens. Ah! is little Kay really dead? The roses have been down in the earth, and they say no."

"Kling! klang!" tolled the Hyacinth Bells. "We are not tolling for little Kay—we don't know him; we only sing our song, the only one we know."

And Gerda went to the Buttercup, gleaming forth from the green leaves.

"You are a little bright sun," said Gerda. "Tell me, if you know, where I may find my companion."

And the Buttercup shone so gaily, and looked back at Gerda. What song might the Buttercup sing? It was not about Kay.

"In a little courtyard the clear sun shone warm on the first day of spring. The sunbeams glided down in the white wall of the neighbouring house; close by grew the first yellow flower, glancing like gold in the bright sun's ray. The old grandmother sat out of doors in her chair; her granddaughter, a poor handsome maidservant, was coming home for a short visit: she kissed her grandmother. There was gold, heart's gold, in that blessed kiss, gold in the mouth, gold in the south, gold in the morning hour. See, that's my little story," said the Buttercup.

"My poor old grandmother!" sighed Gerda. "Yes, she is surely longing for me and grieving for me, just as she did for little Kay. But I shall soon go home and take Kay with me. There is no use of my asking the flowers, they only know their own song, and give me no information." And then she tied her little frock round her, that she might run the faster; but the Jonquil struck against her leg as she sprang over it, and she stopped to look at the tall yellow flower, and asked, "Do you, perhaps, know anything of little Kay?"

And she bent quite down to the flower, and what did it say?

"I can see myself! I can see myself!" said the Jonquil. "Oh! oh! how I can smell! Up in the little room in the gable stands a little dancing girl: she stands sometimes on one foot, sometimes on both; she seems to tread on all the world. She's nothing but an ocular delusion: she pours water out of a teapot on a bit of stuff—it is her bodice. 'Cleanliness is a fine thing,' she says; her white frock hangs on a hook; it has been washed in the teapot too, and dried on the roof: she puts it on and ties her saffron handkerchief round her neck, and the dress looks all the whiter. Point your toes! look how she seems to stand on a stalk. I can see myself! I can see myself!"

"I don't care at all about that," said Gerda. "That is nothing to tell me about."

And then she ran to the end of the garden. The door was locked, but she pressed against the rusty lock, and it broke off, the door sprang open, and little Gerda ran with naked feet out into the wide world. She looked back three times, but no one was there to pursue her; at last she could run no longer, and seated herself on a great stone, and when she looked round the summer was over—it was late in autumn: one could not notice that in the beautiful garden, where there was always sunshine, and the flowers of every season always bloomed.

"Alas! how I have loitered!" said little Gerda. "Autumn has come. I may not rest again."

And she rose up to go on. Oh! how sore and tired her little feet were. All around it looked cold and bleak; the long willow leaves were quite yellow, and the mist dropped from them like water; one leaf after another dropped; only the sloe-thorn still bore fruit, but the sloes were sour, and set the teeth on edge. Oh, how grey and gloomy it looked, the wide world!

FOURTH STORY

THE PRINCE AND PRINCESS

Gerda was compelled to rest again; then there came hopping across the snow, just opposite the spot where she was sitting, a great Crow. This Crow had long been sitting looking at her, nodding its head—now it said, "Krah! krah! Good day! good day!" It could not pronounce better, but it felt friendly towards the little girl, and asked where she was going all alone in the wide world. The word "alone" Gerda understood very well, and felt how much it expressed; and she told the Crow the whole story of her life and fortunes, and asked if it had not seen Kay.

And the Crow nodded very gravely, and said,

"That may be! that may be!"

"What, do you think so?" cried the little girl, and nearly pressed the Crow to death, she kissed it so.

"Gently, gently!" said the Crow. "I think I know: I believe it may be little Kay, but he has certainly forgotten you, with the Princess."

"Does he live with a Princess?" asked Gerda.

"Yes; listen," said the Crow. "But it's so difficult for me to speak your language. If you know the Crow's language, I can tell it much better."

"No, I never learned it," said Gerda; "but my grandmother understood it, and could speak the languages too. I only wish I had learned it."

"That doesn't matter," said the Crow. "I shall tell you as well as I can."

And then the Crow told what he knew.

"In the country in which we now are, lives a Princess who is quite wonderfully clever, but then she has read all the newspapers in the world, and has forgotten them again, she is so clever. Lately she was sitting on the throne—and that's not so pleasant as is generally supposed—and she began to sing a song, and it was just this, 'Why should I not marry now?' You see, there was something in that," said the Crow. "And so she wanted to marry, but she wished for a husband who could answer when he was spoken to, not one who only stood and looked handsome, for that is so tiresome. And so she had all her maids of honour summoned, and when they heard her intention they were very

glad. 'I like that,' said they; 'I thought the very same thing the other day.' You may be sure that every word I am telling you is true," added the Crow. "I have a tame sweetheart who goes about freely in the castle, and she told me everything."

Of course the sweetheart was a crow, for one crow always finds out another, and birds of a feather flock together.

"Newspapers were published directly, with a border of hearts and the Princess's initials. One could read in them that every young man who was good-looking might come to the castle and speak with the Princess, and him who spoke so that one could hear he was at home there, and who spoke best, the Princess would choose for her husband. Yes, yes," said the Crow, "you may believe me. It's as true as I sit here. Young men came flocking in; there was a great crowding and much running to and fro, but no one succeeded the first or second day. They could all speak well when they were out in the streets, but when they entered at the palace gates, and saw the guards standing in their silver lace and went up the staircase, and saw the lackeys in their golden liveries, and the great lighted halls, they became confused. And when they stood before the throne itself, on which the Princess sat, they could do nothing but repeat the last word she had spoken, and she did not care to hear her own words again. It was just as if the people in there had taken some narcotic and fallen asleep, till they got into the street again, for not till then were they able to speak. There stood a whole row of them, from the town gate to the palace gate. I went in myself to see it," said the Crow. "They were hungry and thirsty, but in the palace they did not receive so much as a glass of lukewarm water. A few of the wisest had brought bread and butter with them, but they would not share with their neighbours, for they thought 'Let him look hungry, and the Princess won't have him.'"

"But Kay, little Kay?" asked Gerda. "When did he come? Was he among the crowd?"

"Wait, wait! We're just coming to him. It was on the third day that there came a little personage, without horse or carriage, walking quite merrily up to the castle; his eyes sparkled like yours, he had fine long hair, but his clothes were shabby."

"That was Kay!" cried Gerda, rejoicingly. "Oh, then I have found him!" And she clapped her hands.

"He had a little knapsack on his back," observed the Crow.

"No, that must certainly have been his sledge," said Gerda, "for he went away with a sledge."

"That may well be," said the Crow, "for I did not look to it very closely. But this much I know from my tame sweetheart, that when he passed under the palace gate and saw the Life Guards in silver, and mounted the staircase and saw the lackeys in gold, he was not in the least embarrassed. He nodded, and said to them, 'It must be tedious work standing on the stairs—I'd rather go in.' The halls

shone full of lights; privy councillors and Excellencies walked about with bare feet, and carried golden vessels; any one might have become solemn; and his boots creaked most noisily, but he was not embarrassed."

"That is certainly Kay!" cried Gerda. "He had new boots on; I've heard them creak in grandmother's room."

"Yes, certainly they creaked," resumed the Crow. "And he went boldly to the Princess herself, who sat on a pearl that was as big as a spinning-wheel; and all the maids of honour with their attendants, and the attendants' attendants, and all the cavaliers with their followers, and the followers of their followers, who themselves kept a page apiece, were standing round; and the nearer they stood to the door, the prouder they looked. The followers' followers' pages, who always went in slippers, could hardly be looked at, so proudly did they stand in the doorway!"

"That must be terrible!" faltered little Gerda. "And yet Kay won the Princess?"

"If I had not been a crow, I would have married her myself, notwithstanding that I am engaged. They say he spoke as well as I can speak the crow's language; I heard that from my tame sweetheart. He was merry and agreeable; he had not come to woo, but only to hear the wisdom of the Princess; and he approved of her, and she of him."

"Yes, certainly that was Kay!" said Gerda. "He was so clever, he could do mental arithmetic up to fractions. Oh! won't you lead me to the castle too?"

"That's easily said," replied the Crow. "But how are we to manage it? I'll talk it over with my tame sweetheart; she can probably advise us; for this I must tell you—a little girl like yourself will never get leave to go quite in."

"Yes, I shall get leave," said Gerda. "When Kay hears that I'm there he'll come out directly, and bring me in."

"Wait for me yonder at the stile," said the Crow; and it wagged its head and flew away.

It was already late in the evening when the Crow came back.

"Rare! rare!" it said. "I'm to greet you kindly from my sweetheart, and here's a little loaf for you. She took it from the kitchen. There's plenty of bread there, and you must be hungry. You can't possibly get into the palace, for you are barefoot, and the guards in silver and the lackeys in gold would not allow it. But don't cry; you shall go up. My sweetheart knows a little back staircase that leads up to the bedroom, and she knows where she can get the key."

And they went into the garden, into the great avenue, where one leaf was falling down after another; and when the lights were extinguished in the palace one after the other, the Crow led Gerda to a back door, which stood ajar.

Oh, how Gerda's heart beat with fear and longing! It was just as if she had been going to do something wicked; and yet she only wanted to know if it was little Kay. Yes, it must be he. She thought so deeply of his clear eyes and his long hair, she could fancy she saw how he smiled as he had smiled at home when they sat among the roses. He would certainly be glad to see her; to hear what a long distance she had come for his sake; to know how sorry they had all been at home when he did not come back. Oh, what a fear and what a joy that was!

Now they were on the staircase. A little lamp was burning upon a cupboard, and in the middle of the floor stood the tame Crow turning her head on every side and looking at Gerda, who curtsied as her grandmother had taught her to do.

"My betrothed has spoken to me very favourably of you, my little lady," said the tame Crow. "Your history, as it may be called, is very moving. Will you take the lamp? then I will precede you. We will go the straight way, for we shall meet nobody."

"I feel as if some one were coming after us," said Gerda, as something rushed by her: it seemed like shadows on the wall; horses with flying manes and thin legs, hunters, and ladies and gentlemen on horseback.

"These are only dreams," said the Crow; "they are coming to carry the high masters' thoughts out hunting. That's all the better, for you may look at them the more closely, in bed. But I hope, when you come to honour and dignity, you will show a grateful heart."

"Of that you may be sure!" observed the Crow from the wood.

Now they came into the first hall: it was hung with rose-coloured satin, and artificial flowers were worked on the walls; and here the dreams already came flitting by them, but they moved so quickly that Gerda could not see the high-born lords and ladies. Each hall was more splendid than the last; yes, one could almost become bewildered! Now they were in the bedchamber. Here the ceiling was like a great palm-tree with leaves of glass, of costly glass, and in the middle of the floor two beds hung on a thick stalk of gold, and each of them looked like a lily. One of them was white, and in that lay the Princess; the other was red, and in that Gerda was to seek little Kay. She bent one of the red leaves aside, and then she saw a little brown neck. Oh, that was Kay! She called out his name quite loud, and held the lamp towards him. The dreams rushed into the room again on horseback—he awoke, turned his head, and—it was not little Kay!

The Prince was only like him in the neck! but he was young and good-looking, and the Princess looked up, blinking, from the white lily, and asked who was there. Then little Gerda wept, and told her whole history, and all that the Crows had done for her.

"You poor child!" said the Prince and Princess.

And they praised the Crows, and said that they were not angry with them at all, but the Crows were not to do it again. However they should be rewarded.

"Will you fly out free?" asked the Princess, "or will you

have fixed positions as court crows, with the right to everything that is left in the kitchen?"

And the two Crows bowed, and begged for fixed positions, for they thought of their old age, and said, "It is so good to have some provisions for one's old days," as they called them.

And the Prince got up out of his bed, and let Gerda sleep in it, and he could not do more than that. She folded her little hands, and thought, "How good men and animals are!" and then she shut her eyes and went quietly to sleep. All the dreams came flying in again, looking like angels, and they drew a little sledge, on which Kay sat nodding; but all this was only a dream, and therefore it was gone again as soon as she awoke.

The next day she was clothed from head to foot in silk and velvet; and an offer was made her that she should stay in the castle and enjoy pleasant times; but she only begged for a little carriage, with a horse to draw it, and a pair of little boots; then she would drive out into the world and seek for Kay.

And she received not only boots, but a muff likewise, and was neatly dressed; and when she was ready to depart a coach made of pure gold stopped before the door. Upon it shone like a star the coat of arms of the Prince and Princess; coachman, footmen, and outriders—for there were outriders too—sat on horseback with gold crowns on their heads. The Prince and Princess themselves helped her into the carriage,

151

and wished her all good fortune. The forest Crow, who was now married, accompanied her the first three miles; he sat by Gerda's side, for he could not bear riding backwards: the other Crow stood in the doorway flapping her wings; she did not go with them, for she suffered from headache, that had come on since she had obtained a fixed position and was allowed to eat too much. The coach was lined with sugar-biscuits, and in the seat there were gingerbread-nuts and fruit.

"Farewell, farewell!" cried the Prince and Princess; and little Gerda wept, and the Crow wept. So they went on for the first three miles; and then the Crow said good-bye, and that was the heaviest parting of all. The Crow flew up on a tree, and beat his black wings as long as he could see the coach, which glittered like the bright sunshine.

FIFTH STORY

THE LITTLE ROBBER GIRL

They drove on through the thick forest, but the coach gleamed like a torch, dazzling the robbers' eyes, so that they could not bear it.

"That is gold! that is gold!" cried they, and rushed forward, and seized the horses, killed the postillions, the coachman, and the footmen, and then pulled little Gerda out of the carriage.

"She is fat—she is pretty—she is fed with nut-kernels!" said the old robber woman, who had a very long stiff beard,

and shaggy eyebrows that hung down over her eyes. "She's as good as a little pet lamb; how I shall relish her!"

And she drew out her shining knife, that gleamed in a horrible way.

"Oh!" screamed the old woman at the same moment; for her own daughter who hung at her back bit her ear in a very naughty and spiteful manner. "You ugly brat!" screamed the old woman; and she had not time to kill Gerda.

"She shall play with me!" said the little robber girl. "She shall give me her muff and her pretty dress and sleep with me in my bed!"

And then the girl gave another bite, so that the woman jumped high up and turned right round, and all the robbers laughed and said,

"Look how she dances with her calf."

"I want to go into the carriage," said the little robber girl.

And she would have her own way, for she was spoiled, and very obstinate; and she and Gerda sat in the carriage, and drove over stock and stone deep into the forest. The little robber girl was as big as Gerda, but stronger and more broad-shouldered; and she had a brown skin; her eyes were quite black, and they looked almost mournful. She clasped little Gerda round the waist, and said,

"They shall not kill you as long as I am not angry with you. I suppose you are a Princess?"

"No," replied Gerda. And she told all that had happened to her, and how fond she was of little Kay.

The robber girl looked at her seriously, nodded slightly, and said,

"They shall not kill you even if I do get angry with you, for then I will do it myself."

And then she dried Gerda's eyes, and put her two hands into the beautiful muff that was so soft and warm.

Now the coach stopped, and they were in the courtyard of a robber castle. It had split from the top to the bottom; ravens and crows flew out of the great holes, and big bull-dogs—each of which looked as if he could devour a man—jumped high up, but they did not bark, for that was for-bidden.

In the great old smoky hall a bright fire burned upon the stone floor; the smoke passed along under the ceiling, and had to seek an exit for itself. A great cauldron of soup was boil-ing and hares and rabbits were roasting on the spit.

"You shall sleep to-night with me and all my little ani-mals," said the robber girl.

They got something to eat and drink, and then went to a corner, where straw and carpets were spread out. Above these sat on laths and perches more than a hundred pigeons, that all seemed asleep, but they turned a little when the two girls came.

"All these belong to me," said the little robber girl; and she quickly seized one of the nearest, held it by the feet, and shook it so that it flapped its wings. "Kiss it!" she cried, and beat it in Gerda's face. "There sit the wood rascals," she continued, pointing to a number of laths that had been nailed in front of a hole in the wall. "Those are wood rascals, those two; they fly away directly if one does not keep them well locked up. And here's my old sweetheart 'Ba.' " And she pulled out by the horn a Reindeer, that was tied up, and had a polished copper ring round its neck. "We're obliged to keep him tight, too, or he'd run away from us. Every evening I tickle his neck with a sharp knife, and he's very frightened at that."

And the little girl drew a long knife from a cleft in the wall, and let it glide over the Reindeer's neck; the poor creature kicked out its legs, and the little robber girl laughed, and drew Gerda into bed with her.

"Do you keep the knife beside you while you're asleep?" asked Gerda, and looked at it in rather a frightened way.

"I always sleep with my knife," replied the robber girl. "One does not know what may happen. But now tell me again what you told me just now about little Kay, and why you came out into the wide world."

And Gerda told it again from the beginning; and the Wood Pigeons cooed above them in their cage, and the other pigeons slept. The little robber girl put her arm round Gerda's neck, held her knife in the other hand and slept so that one could hear her; but Gerda could not close her eyes at all—she did not know whether she was to live or die.

The robbers sat round the fire, singing and drinking, and

the old robber woman tumbled about. It was quite terrible for a little girl to behold.

Then the Wood Pigeons said "Coo! coo! we have seen little Kay. A white hen was carrying his sledge: he sat in the Snow Queen's carriage, which drove close by the forest as we lay in our nests. She blew upon us young pigeons, and all died except us two. Coo! coo!"

"What are you saying there?" asked Gerda. "Whither was the Snow Queen travelling? Do you know anything about it?"

"She was probably journeying to Lapland, for there they have always ice and snow. Ask the Reindeer that is tied up with the cord."

"There is ice and snow yonder, and it is glorious and fine," said the Reindeer. "There one may run about free in great glittering plains. There the Snow Queen has her summer tent; but her strong castle is up towards the North Pole, on the island that's called Spitzbergen."

"Oh, Kay, little Kay!" cried Gerda.

"You must lie still," exclaimed the robber girl, "or I shall thrust my knife into your body."

In the morning Gerda told her all that the Wood Pigeons had said, and the robber girl looked quite serious, and nodded her head and said,

"That's all the same, that's all the same!"

"Do you know where Lapland is!" she asked the Reindeer.

"Who should know better than I?" the creature replied, and its eyes sparkled in its head. "I was born and bred there; I ran about there in the snow-fields."

"Listen!" said the robber girl to Gerda. "You see all our men have gone away. Only mother is here still, and she'll stay: but towards noon she drinks out of the big bottle, and then sleeps for a little while; then I'll do something for you."

Then she sprang out of bed, and clasped her mother round the neck and pulled her beard, crying,

"Good morning, my old nanny-goat." And her mother filliped her nose till it was red and blue; but it was all done for pure love.

When the mother had drunk out of her bottle and had gone to sleep upon it, the robber girl went to the Reindeer, and said,

"I should like very much to tickle you a few times more with the knife, for you are very funny then; but it's all the same. I'll loosen your cord and help you out, so that you may run to Lapland; but you must use your legs well, and carry this little girl to the palace of the Snow Queen, where her playfellow is. You've heard what she told me, for she spoke loud enough and you were listening."

The Reindeer sprang up high for joy. The robber girl lifted little Gerda on its back, and had the forethought to tie her fast, and even to give her a little cushion as a saddle.

"There are your fur boots for you," she said, "for it's

THE SNOW QUEEN

growing cold; but I shall keep the muff, for that's so very pretty. Still, you shall not be cold, for all that: here's my mother's big mufflers—they'll just reach up to your elbows. Now your hands look just like my ugly mother's."

And Gerda wept for joy.

"I can't bear to see you whimper," said the little robber girl. "No, you just ought to look very glad. And here are two loaves and a ham for you, so you won't be hungry."

These were tied on the Reindeer's back. The little robber girl opened the door, coaxed in all the big dogs, and then cut the rope with her sharp knife, and said to the Reindeer,

"Now run, but take good care of the little girl."

And Gerda stretched out her hands with the big mufflers towards the little robber girl, and said, "Farewell!"

And the Reindeer ran over stock and stone, away through the great forest, over marshes and steppes, as quick as it could go. The wolves howled and the ravens croaked. "Hiss! hiss!" it went in the air. It seemed as if the sky were flashing fire.

"Those are my old Northern Lights," said the Reindeer. "Look how they glow!" And then it ran on faster than ever, day and night.

The loaves were eaten, and the ham as well, and then they were in Lapland.

SIXTH STORY

THE LAPLAND WOMAN AND THE FINLAND WOMAN

At a little hut they stopped. It was very humble; the roof sloped down almost to the ground, and the door was so low that the family had to creep on their stomachs when they wanted to go in or out. No one was in the house but an old Lapland woman, cooking fish on a train-oil lamp; and the Reindeer told Gerda's whole history, but it related its own first, for this seemed to the Reindeer the most important of the two. Gerda was so exhausted by the cold that she could not speak.

"Oh, you poor things," said the Lapland woman, "you've a long way to run yet! You must go more than a hundred miles into Finmark, for the Snow Queen is there, staying in the country, and burning Bengal lights every evening. I'll write a few words on a dried cod, for I have no paper, and I'll give you that as a letter to the Finland woman; she can give you better information than I."

And when Gerda had been warmed and refreshed with food and drink, the Lapland woman wrote a few words on a dried codfish, and telling Gerda to take care of it, tied her again on the Reindeer and the Reindeer sprang away. Flash! flash! it went high in the air; the whole night long the most beautiful blue Northern Lights were burning.

And then they got to Finmark, and knocked at the chimney of the Finland woman, for she had not even a door.

159

THE SNOW QUEEN

There was such a heat in the chimney that the woman herself went about almost naked. She was little and very dirty. She at once loosened little Gerda's dress and took off the child's mufflers and boots; otherwise it would have been too hot for her to bear. Then she laid a piece of ice on the Reindeer's head, and read what was written on the codfish; she read it three times, and when she knew it by heart, she popped the fish into the soup-cauldron, for it was eatable, and she never wasted anything.

Now the Reindeer first told his own history, and then little Gerda's; and the Finland woman blinked with her clever eyes, but said nothing.

"You are very clever," said the Reindeer: "I know you can tie all the winds of the world together with a bit of twine: if the seaman unties one knot, he has a good wind; if he loosens the second, it blows hard; but if he unties the third and the fourth, there comes such a tempest that the forests are thrown down. Won't you give the little girl a draught, so that she may get twelve men's power, and overcome the Snow Queen?"

"Twelve men's power!" repeated the Finland woman. "Great use that would be!"

And she went to a shelf, and brought out a great roll-up fur, and unrolled it; wonderful characters were written upon it and the Finland woman read until the water ran down over her forehead.

But the Reindeer again begged so hard for little Gerda,

and Gerda looked at the Finland woman with such beseeching eyes full of tears, that she began to blink again with her own, and drew the Reindeer into a corner, and whispered to him, while she laid fresh ice upon his head.

"Little Kay is certainly at the Snow Queen's, and finds everything there to his taste and liking, and thinks it the best place in the world; but that is because he has a splinter of glass in his eye, and a little fragment in his heart; but these must be got out, or he will never be a human being again, and the Snow Queen will keep her power over him."

"But cannot you give something to little Gerda, so as to give her power over all this?"

"I can give her no greater power than she possesses already: don't you see how great that is? Don't you see how men and animals are obliged to serve her, and how she gets on so well in the world, with her naked feet? She must not learn her power from us: it consists in this, that she is a dear innocent child. If she herself cannot penetrate to the Snow Queen and get the glass out of little Kay, we can be of no use! Two miles from here the Snow Queen's garden begins; you can carry the little girl thither: set her down by the great bush that stands with its red berries in the snow. Don't stand gossiping, but make haste, and get back here!"

And then the Finland woman lifted little Gerda on the Reindeer, which ran as fast as it could.

"Oh, I haven't my boots! I haven't my mufflers!" cried Gerda.

She soon noticed that in the cutting cold; but the Reindeer dare not stop: it ran till it came to the bush with the red berries; there it set Gerda down, and kissed her on the mouth, and great bright tears ran over the creature's cheeks; and then it ran back, as fast as it could. There stood poor Gerda without shoes, without gloves, in the midst of the terrible cold Finmark.

She ran forward as fast as possible! then came a whole regiment of snowflakes; but they did not fall down from the sky, for that was quite bright, and shone with the Northern Lights: the snowflakes ran along the ground, and the nearer they came the larger they grew. Gerda still remembered how large and beautiful the snowflakes had appeared when she looked at them through the burning-glass. But here they were certainly far longer and much more terrible—they were alive. They were the advanced posts of the Snow Queen, and had the strangest shapes. A few looked like ugly great porcupines; others like knots formed of snakes, which stretched forth their heads; and others like little fat bears, whose hair stood on end: all were brilliantly white, all were living snowflakes.

Then little Gerda said her prayer; and the cold was so great that she could see her own breath, which went forth out of her mouth like smoke. The breath became thicker and thicker, and formed itself into little angels, who grew and grew whenever they touched the earth; and all had helmets on their heads and shields and spears in their hands;

their number increased more and more, and when Gerda had finished her prayer a whole legion stood round about her and struck with their spears at the terrible snowflakes, so that these were shattered into a thousand pieces; and little Gerda could go forward afresh, with good courage. The angels stroked her hands and feet, and then she felt less how cold it was, and hastened on to the Snow Queen's palace.

But now we must see what Kay is doing. He certainly was not thinking of little Gerda, and least of all that she was standing in front of the palace.

SEVENTH STORY

OF THE SNOW QUEEN'S CASTLE AND WHAT HAPPENED THERE AT LAST

The walls of the palace were formed of the drifting snow, and the windows and doors of the cutting winds. There were more than a hundred halls, all blown together by the snow: the greatest of these extended for several miles; the strong Northern Lights illumined them all, and how great and empty, how icily cold and shining they all were! Never was merriment there, not even a little bears' ball, at which the storm could have played the music, while the bears walked about on their hind legs and showed off their pretty manners; never any little coffee gossip among the young lady white foxes. Empty, vast, and cold were the halls of the Snow Queen. The Northern Lights flamed so brightly that

one could count them where they stood highest and lowest. In the midst of this immense empty snow hall was a frozen lake, which had burst into a thousand pieces; but each piece was like the rest, so that it was a perfect work of art; and in the middle of the lake sat the Snow Queen when she was at home, and then she said that she sat in the mirror of reason, and that this was the only one, and the best in the world.

Little Kay was quite blue with cold—indeed, almost black, but he did not notice it, for she had kissed the cold shudderings away from him; and his heart was like a lump of ice. He dragged a few sharp flat pieces of ice to and fro, joining them together in all kinds of ways, for he wanted to achieve something with them. It was just like when we have little tablets of wood, and lay them together to form figures —what we call the Chinese puzzle. Kay also went and laid figures, and, indeed, very artistic ones. That was the icy game of reason. In his eyes these figures were very remarkable and of the highest importance; that was because of the fragment of glass sticking in his eye. He laid out the figures so that they formed a word—but he could never manage to lay down the word as he wished to have it— the word "Eternity." And the Snow Queen had said,

"If you can find out this figure, you shall be your own master, and I will give you the whole world and a new pair of skates."

But he could not.

But Gerda and Kay went hand in hand,
and as they went it became beautiful
Spring, with green and wild flowers.

[See Page 170]

"Now I'll hasten away to the warm lands," said the Snow Queen. "I will go and look into the black pots": these were the volcanoes, Etna and Vesuvius, as they are called. "I shall make them a little white! That's necessary; that will do the grapes and lemons good."

And the Snow Queen flew away, and Kay sat quite alone in the great icy hall that was miles in extent, and looked at his pieces of ice, and thought so deeply that cracks were heard inside him: he sat quite stiff and still; one would have thought that he was frozen to death.

Then it happened that little Gerda stepped through the great gate into the wide hall. Here reigned cutting winds, but she prayed a prayer, and the winds lay down as if they would have gone to sleep; and she stepped into the great empty cold halls, and beheld Kay; she knew him, and flew to him and embraced him, and held him fast, and called out,

"Kay, dear little Kay! at last I have found you!"

But he sat quite still, stiff and cold. Then little Gerda wept hot tears, that fell upon his breast; they penetrated into his heart, they thawed the lump of ice, and consumed the little piece of glass in it. He looked at her, and she sang:

> Roses bloom and roses decay,
> But we the Christ-child shall see one day.

Then Kay burst into tears; he wept so that the splinter of glass came out of his eye. Now he recognised her and cried rejoicingly,

"Gerda, dear Gerda! where have you been all this time? And where have I been?" And he looked all around him. "How cold it is here! how large and empty!"

And he clung to Gerda, and she laughed and wept for joy. It was so glorious that even the pieces of ice round about danced for joy; and when they were tired and lay down, they formed themselves just into the letters of which the Snow Queen had said that if he found them out he should be his own master, and she would give him the whole world and a new pair of skates.

And Gerda kissed his cheeks, and they became blooming; she kissed his eyes, and they shone like her own; she kissed his hands and feet, and he became well and merry. The Snow Queen might now come home; his letter of release stood written in shining characters of ice.

And they took one another by the hand, and wandered forth from the great palace of ice. They spoke of the grandmother, and of the roses on the roof; and where they went the winds rested and the sun burst forth; and when they came to the bush with the red berries, the Reindeer was standing there waiting: it had brought another young reindeer, which gave the children warm milk, and kissed them on the mouth. Then they carried Kay and Gerda, first to the Finnish woman, where they warmed themselves thoroughly in the hot room, and received instructions for their journey home, and then to the Lapland woman, who had made their new clothes and put their sledge in order.

The Reindeer and the young one sprang at their side, and followed them as far as the boundary of the country. There the first green sprouted forth, and there they took leave of the two reindeer and the Lapland woman. "Farewell!" said all. And the first little birds began to twitter, the forest was decked with green buds and out of it on a beautiful horse (which Gerda knew, for it was the same that had drawn her golden coach) a young girl came riding, with a shining red cap on her head and a pair of pistols in the holsters. This was the little robber girl, who had grown tired of staying at home, and wished to go first to the north, and if that did not suit her, to some other region. She knew Gerda at once, and Gerda knew her too; and it was a right merry meeting. "You are a fine fellow to gad about!" she said to little Kay. "I should like to know if you deserve that one should run to the end of the world after you?"

But Gerda patted her cheeks, and asked after the Prince and Princess.

"They've gone to foreign countries," said the robber girl.

"But the Crow?"

"Why, the Crow is dead," answered the other. "The tame one has become a widow, and goes about with an end of black worsted thread round her leg. She complains most lamentably, but it's all talk. But now tell me how you have fared, and how you caught him."

And Gerda and Kay told their story.

"Snip-snap-snurre-basse-lurre!" said the robber girl.

And she took them both by the hand and promised that if she ever came through their town, she would come up and pay them a visit. And then she rode away into the wide world. But Gerda and Kay went hand in hand, and as they went it became beautiful spring, with green and with flowers. The church bells sounded, and they recognised the high steeples and the great town: it was the one in which they lived; and they went to the grandmother's door, and up the stairs, and into the room, where everything remained in its usual place. The big clock was going "Tick! tack!" and the hands were turning; but as they went through the rooms they noticed that they had become grown-up people. The roses out on the roof gutter were blooming in at the open window, and there stood the little children's chairs, and Kay and Gerda sat each upon their own, and held each other by the hand. They had forgotten the cold empty splendour at the Snow Queen's like a heavy dream. The grandmother was sitting in God's bright sunshine, and read aloud out of the Bible, "Except ye become as little children, ye shall in no wise enter into the kingdom of God."

And Kay and Gerda looked into each other's eyes, and all at once they understood the old hymn—

> Roses bloom and roses decay,
> But we the Christ-child shall see one day.

There they both sat, grown up, and yet children—children in heart—and it was summer, warm, delightful summer.

THE · RED · SHOES

THE RED SHOES

HERE was once a little girl; a very nice pretty little girl. But in summer she had to go barefoot, because she was poor, and in winter she wore thick wooden shoes, so that her little instep became quite red, altogether red.

In the middle of the village lived an old shoemaker's wife: she sat and sewed, as well as she could, a pair of little shoes, of old strips of red cloth; they were clumsy enough, but well meant, and the little girl was to have them. The little girl's name was Karen.

On the day when her mother was buried she received the red shoes and wore them for the first time. They were certainly not suited for mourning; but she had no others, and therefore thrust her little bare feet into them and walked behind the plain deal coffin.

Suddenly a great carriage came by, and in the carriage sat an old lady: she looked at the little girl and felt pity for her, and said to the clergyman,

THE RED SHOES

"Give me the little girl, and I will provide for her."

Karen thought this was for the sake of the shoes; but the old lady declared they were hideous; and they were burned. But Karen herself was clothed neatly and properly: she was taught to read and to sew, and the people said she was agreeable. But her mirror said, "You are much more than agreeable; you are beautiful."

Once the Queen travelled through the country, and had her little daughter with her; and the daughter was a Princess. And the people flocked towards the castle, and Karen, too, was among them; and the little Princess stood in a fine white dress at a window, and let herself be gazed at. She had neither train nor golden crown, but she wore splendid red morocco shoes; they were certainly far handsomer than those the shoemaker's wife had made for little Karen. Nothing in the world can compare with red shoes!

Now Karen was old enough to be confirmed: new clothes were made for her, and she was to have new shoes. The rich shoemaker in the town took the measure of her little feet; this was done in his own house, in his little room, and there stood great glass cases with neat shoes and shining boots. It had quite a charming appearance, but the old lady could not see well, and therefore took no pleasure in it. Among the shoes stood a red pair, just like those which the Princess had worn. How beautiful they were! The shoemaker also said they had been made for a Count's child, but they had not fitted.

"That must be patent leather," observed the old lady, "the shoes shine so!"

"Yes, they shine!" replied Karen; and they fitted her, and were bought. But the old lady did not know that they were red; for she would never have allowed Karen to go to her confirmation in red shoes; but that is what Karen did.

Every one was looking at her shoes. And when she went up the floor of the church, towards the door of the choir, it seemed to her as if the old figures on the tombstones, the portraits of clergymen and clergymen's wives, in their stiff collars and long black garments, fixed their eyes upon her red shoes. And she thought of her shoes only, when the priest laid his hand upon her head and spoke holy words. And the organ pealed solemnly, the children sang with their fresh sweet voices, and the old precentor sang too; but Karen thought only of her red shoes.

In the afternoon the old lady was informed by every one that the shoes were red; and she said it was naughty and unsuitable, and that when Karen went to Church in future, she should always go in black shoes, even if they were old.

Next Sunday was Sacrament Sunday. And Karen looked at the black shoes, and looked at the red ones—looked at them again—and put on the red ones.

The sun shone gloriously; Karen and the old lady went along the footpath through the fields, and it was rather dusty.

By the Church door stood an old invalid soldier with a crutch and a long beard; the beard was rather red than white, for it was red altogether; and he bowed down almost to the ground, and asked the old lady if he might dust her shoes. And Karen also stretched out her little foot.

"Look, what pretty dancing-shoes!" said the old soldier. "Fit so tightly when you dance!"

And he tapped the soles with his hand. And the old lady gave the soldier an alms, and went into the church with Karen.

And every one in the church looked at Karen's red shoes, and all the pictures looked at them. And while Karen knelt in the church she only thought of her red shoes; and she forgot to sing her psalm, and forgot to say her prayer.

Now all the people went out of church, and the old lady stepped into her carriage. Karen lifted up her foot to step in too; then the old soldier said,

"Look, what beautiful dancing-shoes!"

And Karen could not resist: she was obliged to dance a few steps, and when she once began, her legs went on dancing. It was just as though the shoes had obtained power over her. She danced round the corner of the church—she could not help it; the coachman was obliged to run behind her and seize her: he lifted her into the carriage, but her feet went on dancing, so that she kicked the good old lady violently. At last they took off her shoes, and her legs became quiet.

At home the shoes were put away in a cupboard; but Karen could not resist looking at them.

Now the old lady became very ill, and it was said she would not recover. She had to be nursed and waited on; and this was no one's duty so much as Karen's. But there was to be a great ball in the town, and Karen was invited. She looked at the old lady who could not recover; she looked at the red shoes, and thought there would be no harm in it. She put on the shoes, and that she might very well do; but then she went to the ball and began to dance.

But when she wished to go to the right hand, the shoes danced to the left, and when she wanted to go upstairs the shoes danced downwards, down into the street and out at the town gate. She danced, and was obliged to dance, straight out into the dark wood.

There was something glistening up among the trees, and she thought it was the moon, for she saw a face. But it was the old soldier with the red beard; he sat and nodded, and said,

"Look, what beautiful dancing-shoes!"

Then she was frightened, and wanted to throw away the red shoes; but they clung fast to her. And she tore off her stockings; but the shoes had grown fast to her feet. And she danced and was compelled to go dancing over field and meadow, in rain and sunshine, by night and by day; but it was most dreadful at night.

She danced into the open churchyard; but the dead there did not dance; they had something better to do. She wished to sit down on the poor man's grave, where the bitter tansy

grows; but there was no peace nor rest for her. And when she danced towards the open church door, she saw there an angel in long white garments, with wings that reached from his shoulders to his feet; his countenance was serious and stern, and in his hand he held a sword that was broad and gleaming.

"Thou shalt dance!" he said—"dance in thy red shoes, till thou art pale and cold, and till thy body shrivels to a skeleton. Thou shalt dance from door to door; and where proud, haughty children dwell, shalt thou knock, that they may hear thee, and be afraid of thee! Thou shalt dance, dance!"

"Mercy!" cried Karen.

But she did not hear what the angel answered, for the shoes carried her away—carried her through the gate on to the field, over stock and stone, and she was always obliged to dance.

One morning she danced past a door which she knew well. There was a sound of psalm-singing within and a coffin was carried out, adorned with flowers. Then she knew that the old lady was dead, and she felt that she was deserted by all, and condemned by the angel of God.

She danced, and was compelled to dance—to dance in the dark night. The shoes carried her on over thorn and brier; she scratched herself till she bled; she danced away across the heath to a little lonely house. Here she knew the executioner dwelt; and she tapped with her fingers on the panes, and called,

"Come out, come out! I cannot come in, for I must dance!"

And the executioner said,

"You probably don't know who I am? I cut off the bad people's heads with my axe, and mark how my axe rings!"

"Do not strike off my head," said Karen, "for if you do I cannot repent of my sin. But strike off my feet with the red shoes!"

And then she confessed all her sin, and the executioner cut off her feet with the red shoes; but the shoes danced away with the little feet over the fields and into the deep forest.

And he cut her a pair of wooden feet, with crutches, and taught her a psalm, which the criminals always sing; and she kissed the hand that had held the axe, and went away across the heath.

"Now I have suffered pain enough for the red shoes," said she. "Now I will go into the church, that they may see me."

And she went quickly towards the church door; but when she came there the red shoes danced before her, so that she was frightened, and turned back.

The whole week through she was sorrowful, and wept many bitter tears; but when Sunday came, she said,

THE RED SHOES

"Now I have suffered and striven enough! I think that I am just as good as many of those who sit in the church and carry their heads high."

And then she went boldly on; but she did not get farther than the churchyard gate before she saw the red shoes dancing along before her; then she was seized with terror, and turned back, and repented of her sin right heartily.

And she went to the parsonage, and begged to be taken there as a servant. She promised to be industrious, and to do all she could; she did not care for wages, and only wished to be under a roof and with good people. The clergyman's wife pitied her and took her into her service. And she was industrious and thoughtful. Silently she sat and listened when in the evening the pastor read the Bible aloud. All the little ones were very fond of her; but when they spoke of dress and splendour and beauty she would shake her head.

Next Sunday they all went to church, and she was asked if she wished to go too; but she looked sadly, with tears in her eyes, at her crutches. And then the others went to hear God's Word; but she went alone into her little room, which was only large enough to contain her bed and a chair. And here she sat with her hymn-book; and as she read it with a pious mind, the wind bore the notes of the organ over to her from the church; and she lifted up her face, wet with tears, and said,

"O Lord, help me!"

Then the sun shone so brightly; and before her stood the

angel in white garments, the same she had seen that night at the church door. But he no longer grasped the sharp sword: he held a green branch covered with roses; and he touched the ceiling, and it rose up high, and wherever he touched it a golden star gleamed forth; and he touched the walls, and they spread forth widely, and she saw the organ which was pealing its rich sounds; and she saw the old pictures of clergymen and their wives; and the congregation sat in the decorated seats, and sang from their hymn-books. The church had come to the poor girl in her narrow room, or her chamber had become a church. She sat in the pew with the rest of the clergyman's people; and when they had finished the psalm and looked up, they nodded and said:

"That was right, that you came here, Karen."

"It was mercy!" said she.

And the organ sounded its glorious notes; and the children's voices singing in chorus sounded sweet and lovely; the clear sunshine streamed so warm through the window upon the chair in which Karen sat; and her heart became so filled with sunshine, peace and joy, that it broke. Her soul flew on the sunbeams to heaven; and there was nobody who asked after the RED SHOES.

THE · SHEPHERDESS · AND · THE · CHIMNEY · SWEEP

THE SHEPHERDESS AND THE CHIMNEY-SWEEPER

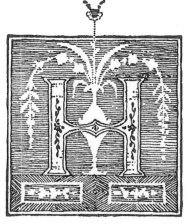

HAVE you ever seen a very old wooden cupboard, quite black with age, and ornamented with carved foliage and arabesques? Just such a cupboard stood in a parlour: it had been a legacy from the great-grandmother, and was covered from top to bottom with carved roses and tulips. There were the quaintest flourishes upon it, and from among these peered forth little stags' heads with antlers. In the middle of the cupboard door an entire figure of a man had been cut out: he was certainly ridiculous to look at, and he grinned, for you could not call it laughing: he had goat's legs, little horns on his head, and a long beard. The children in the room always called him the Billygoat-legs-Lieutenant-and-Major-General-War-Commander-Sergeant; that was a difficult name to pronounce, and there are not many who obtain this title; but it was something to have cut him out. And there he was! He was always looking at the table under the mirror, for on

185

this table stood a lovely little Shepherdess made of china. Her shoes were gilt, her dress was neatly caught up with a red rose, and besides this she had a golden hat and a shepherd's crook: she was very lovely. Close by her stood a little Chimney-Sweeper, black as a coal, but also made of porcelain: he was as clean and neat as any other man, for it was only make-believe that he was a sweep; the china-workers might just as well have made a prince of him, if they had been so minded.

There he stood very nattily with his ladder, and with a face as white and pink as a girl's; and that was really a fault, for he ought to have been a little black. He stood quite close to the Shepherdess; they had both been placed where they stood; but as they had been placed there they had become engaged to each other. They suited each other well. Both were young people, both made of the same kind of china, and both equally frail.

Close to them stood another figure, three times greater than they. This was an old Chinaman, who could nod. He was also of porcelain, and declared himself to be the grandfather of the little Shepherdess; but he could not prove his relationship. He declared he had authority over her, and that, therefore, he had nodded to Mr. Billygoat-legs-Lieutenant-and-Major-General-War-Commander-Sergeant, who was wooing her for his wife.

"Then you will get a husband!" said the old Chinaman, "a man who I verily believe is made of mahogany. He

can make you a Billygoat-legs-Lieutenant-and-Major-General-War-Commander-Sergeantess; he has the whole cupboard full of silver plate, besides what he hoards up in secret drawers."

"I won't go into the dark cupboard!" said the little Shepherdess. "I have heard tell that he has eleven porcelain wives in there."

"Then you may become the twelfth," cried the Chinaman. "This night, so soon as it creaks in the old cupboard, you shall be married, as true as I am an old Chinaman!"

And with that he nodded his head and fell asleep. But the little Shepherdess wept and looked at her heart's beloved, the porcelain Chimney-Sweeper.

"I should like to beg of you," said she, "to go out with me into the wide world, for we cannot remain here."

"I'll do whatever you like," replied the little Chimney-Sweeper. "Let us start directly! I think I can keep you by exercising my profession."

"If we were only safely down from the table!" said she. "I shall not be happy until we are out in the wide world."

And he comforted her, and showed her how she must place her little foot upon the carved corners and the gilded foliage down the leg of the table; he brought his ladder, too, to help her, and they were soon together upon the floor. But when they looked up at the old cupboard there was great commotion within: all the carved stags were stretching out their heads, rearing up their antlers, and turning their necks; and the Billygoat-legs-Lieutenant-and-Major-General-War-

Commander-Sergeant sprang high in the air, and called across to the old Chinaman,

"Now they're running away! now they're running away!"

Then they were a little frightened, and jumped quickly into the drawer of the window-seat. Here were three or four packs of cards which were not complete, and a little puppet-show, which had been built up as well as it could be done. There plays were acted, and all the ladies, diamonds, clubs, hearts, and spades, sat in the first row, fanning themselves with their tulips; and behind them stood all the knaves, showing that they had a head above and below, as is usual in playing cards. The play was about two people who were not to be married to each other, and the Shepherdess wept, because it was just like her own history.

"I cannot bear this!" said she. "I must go out of the drawer."

But when they arrived on the floor, and looked up at the table, the old Chinaman was awake and was shaking over his whole body—for below he was all one lump.

"Now the old Chinaman's coming!" cried the little Shepherdess; and she fell down upon her porcelain knee, so startled was she.

"I have an idea," said the Chimney-Sweeper. "Shall we creep into the great *pot-pourri* vase which stands in the corner? Then we can lie on roses and lavender and throw salt in his eyes if he comes."

"That will be of no use," she replied. "Besides, I know

that the old Chinaman and the *pot-pourri* vase were once engaged to each other, and a kind of liking always remains when people have stood in such a relation to each other. No, there's nothing left for us but to go out into the wide world."

"Have you really courage to go in the wide world with me?" asked the Chimney-Sweeper. "Have you considered how wide the world is, and that we can never come back here again?"

"I have," replied she.

And the Chimney-Sweeper looked fondly at her, and said,

"My way is through the chimney. If you have really courage to creep with me through the stove—through the iron fire-box as well as up the pipe, then we can get out into the chimney, and I know how to find my way through there. We'll mount so high that they can't catch us, and quite at the top there's a hole that leads out into the wide world."

And he led her to the door of the stove.

"It looks very black there," said she; but still she went with him, through the box and through the pipe, where it was pitch-dark night.

"Now we are in the chimney," said he; "and look, look! up yonder a beautiful star is shining."

And it was a real star in the sky, which shone straight down upon them, as if it would show them the way. And they clambered and crept: it was a frightful way, and terribly steep; but he supported her and helped her up; he held her, and showed her the best places where she could place her

little porcelain feet; and thus they reached the edge of the chimney, and upon that they sat down, for they were desperately tired, as they well might be.

The sky with all its stars was high above, and all the roofs of the town deep below them. They looked far around —far, far out into the world. The poor Shepherdess had never thought of it as it really was: she leaned her little head against the Chimney-Sweeper, then she wept so bitterly that the gold ran down off her girdle.

"That is too much," she said. "I cannot bear that. The world is too large! If I were only back upon the table below the mirror! I shall never be happy until I am there again. Now I have followed you out into the wide world, you may accompany me back again if you really love me."

And the Chimney-Sweeper spoke sensibly to her—spoke of the old Chinaman and of the Billygoat-legs-Lieutenant-and-Major-General-War-Commander-Sergeant; but she sobbed bitterly and kissed her little Chimney-Sweeper, so that he could not help giving way to her, though it was foolish.

And so with much labour they climbed down the chimney again. And they crept through the pipe and the fire-box. That was not pleasant at all. And there they stood in the dark stove; there they listened behind the door, to find out what was going on in the room. Then it was quite quiet: they looked in—ah! there lay the old Chinaman in the middle of the floor! He had fallen down from the table as he was pursuing them, and now he lay broken into

"We'll mount so high that they can't catch
us, and quite at the top there's a hole
that leads out into the wide world."

[See Page 189]

three pieces; his back had come off all in one piece, and his head had rolled into a corner. The Billygoat-legs-Lieutenant-and-Major-General-War-Commander-Sergeant stood where he had always stood, considering.

"That is terrible!" said the little Shepherdess. "The old grandfather has fallen to pieces, and it is our fault. I shall never survive it!" And then she wrung her little hands. "He can be mended! he can be mended!" said the Chimney-Sweeper. "Don't be so violent. If they glue his back together and give him a good rivet in his neck he will be as good as new, and may say many a disagreeable thing to us yet."

"Do you think so?" cried she.

So they climbed back upon the table where they used to stand.

"You see, we have come back to this," said the Chimney-Sweeper: "we might have saved ourselves all the trouble we have had."

"If the old grandfather were only riveted!" said the Shepherdess. "I wonder if that is dear?"

And he was really riveted. The family had his back cemented, and a great rivet was passed through his neck: he was as good as new, only he could no longer nod.

"It seems you have become proud since you fell to pieces," said the Billygoat-legs-Lieutenant-and-Major-General-War-Commander-Sergeant. "I don't think you have any reason to give yourself such airs. Am I to have her or am I not?"

And the Chimney-Sweeper and the little Shepherdess looked at the old Chinaman most piteously, for they were afraid he might nod. But he could not do that, and it was irksome to him to tell a stranger that he always had a rivet in his neck. And so the porcelain people remained together, and they blessed Grandfather's rivet, and loved one another until they broke.

THE · SHADOW

THE SHADOW

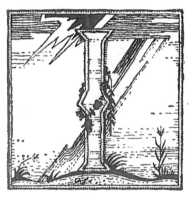N the hot countries the sun burns very strongly; there the people become quite mahogany brown, and in the very hottest countries they are even burned into negroes. But this time it was only to the hot countries that a learned man out of the cold regions had come. He thought he could roam about there just as he had been accustomed to do at home; but he soon altered his opinion. He and all sensible people had to remain at home, where the window-shutters and doors were shut all day long, and it looked as if all the inmates were asleep or had gone out. The narrow street with the high houses in which he lived was, however, built in such a way that the sun shone upon it from morning till evening; it was really quite unbearable! The learned man from the cold regions was a young man and a clever man: it seemed to him as if he was sitting in a glowing oven that exhausted him greatly, and he became quite thin; even his shadow shrivelled up and became much smaller than it had been at home; the sun even told upon it, and it did not recover till the evening, when the sun

went down. It was really a pleasure to see this. So soon as a light was brought into the room the Shadow stretched itself quite up the wall, farther even than the ceiling, so tall did it make itself; it was obliged to stretch to get strength again. The learned man went out into the balcony to stretch himself, and as soon as the stars came out in the beautiful clear sky, he felt himself reviving. On all the balconies in the streets—and in the hot countries there is a balcony to every window—people now appeared, for one must breathe fresh air, even if one has got used to being mahogany; then it became lively above and below; the shoemakers and tailors and everybody sat below in the street; then tables and chairs were brought out, and candles burned, yes, more than a thousand candles; one talked and another sang, and the people walked to and fro; carriages drove past, mules trotted, "Kling-ling-ling!" for they had bells on their harness; dead people were buried with solemn songs; the church bells rang, and it was indeed very lively in the street. Only in one house, just opposite to that in which the learned man dwelt, it was quite quiet, and yet somebody lived there, for there were flowers upon the balcony, blooming beautifully in the hot sun, and they could not have done this if they had not been watered, so that some one must have watered them; therefore, there must be people in that house. Towards evening the door was half opened, but it was dark, at least in the front room; further back, in the interior, music was heard. The strange learned man thought this music very lovely, but it was quite possible that he only imagined this, for out there in the hot countries he found everything exquisite, if only there had been no sun. The stranger's landlord said that he did not know who had taken the opposite house—one saw nobody there, and so far as the music was concerned, it seemed very monotonous to him.

"It was just," he said, "as if some one sat there, always practising a piece that he could not manage—always the same piece. He seemed to say, 'I shall manage it, after all'; but he did not manage it, however long he played."

The stranger was asleep one night. He slept with the balcony door open: the wind lifted up the curtain before it, and he fancied that a wonderful radiance came from the balcony of the house opposite; all the flowers appeared like flames of the most gorgeous colours, and in the midst, among the flowers, stood a beautiful slender maiden: it seemed as if a radiance came from her also. His eyes were quite dazzled; but he had only opened them too wide just when he awoke out of his sleep. With one leap he was out of bed; quite quietly he crept behind the curtain; but the maiden was gone, the splendour was gone, the flowers gleamed no longer, but stood there as beautiful as ever. The door was ajar, and from within sounded music, so lovely, so charming, that one fell into sweet thought at the sound. It was just like magic work. But who lived there? Where was the real entrance? for towards the street and towards

199

the lane at the side the whole ground floor was shop by shop, and the people could not always run through there.

One evening the stranger sat up on his balcony; in the room just behind him a light was burning, and so it was quite natural that his Shadow fell upon the wall of the opposite house; yes, it sat just among the flowers on the balcony, and when the stranger moved his Shadow moved too.

"I think my Shadow is the only living thing we see yonder," said the learned man. "Look how gracefully it sits among the flowers. The door is only ajar, but the Shadow ought to be sensible enough to walk in and look round, and then come back and tell me what it has seen."

"Yes, you would thus make yourself very useful," said he, in sport. "Be so good as to slip in. Now, will you go?" And then he nodded at the Shadow, and the Shadow nodded back at him. "Now go, but don't stay away altogether."

And the stranger stood up, and the Shadow on the balcony opposite stood up too, and the stranger turned round, and the Shadow turned also, and if any one had noticed closely he would have remarked how the Shadow went away in the same moment, straight through the half-opened door of the opposite house, as the stranger returned into his room and let the curtain fall.

Next morning the learned man went out to drink coffee and read the papers.

THE SHADOW

"What is this?" said he, when he came out into the sunshine. "I have no Shadow! So it really went away yesterday evening, and did not come back: that's very tiresome."

And that fretted him, but not so much because the Shadow was gone as because he knew that there was a story of a man without a shadow. All the people in the cold lands knew this story, and if the learned man came home and told his own history, they would say that it was only an imitation, and he did not choose that they should say this of him. So he would not speak of it at all, and that was a very sensible idea of his.

In the evening he again went out on his balcony: he had placed the light behind him, for he knew that a shadow always wants its master for a screen, but he could not coax it forth. He made himself little, he made himself long, but there was no shadow, and no shadow came. He said, "Here, here!" but that did no good.

That was vexatious, but in the warm countries everything grows very quickly, and after the lapse of a week he remarked to his great joy that a new shadow was growing out of his legs when he went into the sunshine, so that the root must have remained behind. After three weeks he had quite a respectable shadow, which, when he started on his return to the North, grew more and more, so that at last it was so long and great that he could very well have parted with half of it.

THE SHADOW

When the learned man got home he wrote books about what is true in the world, and what is good, and what is pretty; and days went by, and years went by, many years.

He was one evening sitting in his room when there came a little quiet knock at the door. "Come in!" said he; but nobody came. Then he opened the door, and there stood before him such a remarkably thin man that he felt quite uncomfortable. This man was, however, very respectably dressed; he looked like a man of standing.

"Whom have I the honour to address?" asked the professor.

"Ah!" replied the genteel man, "I thought you would not know me; I have become so much a body that I have got real flesh and clothes. You never thought to see me in such a condition. Don't you know your old Shadow? You certainly never thought that I would come again. Things have gone remarkably well with me since I was with you last. I've become rich in every respect: if I want to buy myself free from servitude I can do it!"

And he rattled a number of valuable charms, which hung by his watch, and put his hand upon the thick gold chain he wore round his neck; and how the diamond rings glittered on his fingers! and everything was real!

"No, I cannot regain my self-possession at all!" said the learned man. "What's the meaning of all this?"

"Nothing common," said the Shadow. "But you, yourself, don't belong to common folks; and I have, as you very well know, trodden in your footsteps from my childhood upwards. So soon as you thought that I was experienced enough to find my way through the world alone, I went away. I am in the most brilliant circumstances; but I was seized with a kind of longing to see you once more before you die, and I wanted to see these regions once more, for one always thinks much of one's fatherland. I know that you have got another shadow: have I anything to pay to it, or to you? You have only to tell me."

"Is it really you?" said the learned man. "Why, that is wonderful! I should never have thought that I should ever meet my old Shadow as a man!"

"Only tell me what I have to pay," said the Shadow, "for I don't like to be in any one's debt."

"How can you talk in that way?" said the learned man. "Of what debt can there be a question here? You are as free as any one! I am exceedingly pleased at your good fortune! Sit down, old friend, and tell me a little how it has happened, and what you saw in the warm countries, and in the house opposite ours."

"Yes, that I will tell you," said the Shadow; and it sat down. "But then you must promise me never to tell any one in this town, when you meet me, that I have ever been your Shadow! I have the intention of engaging myself to be married; I can do more than support a family."

"Be quite easy," replied the learned man; "I will tell

nobody who you really are. Here's my hand. I promise it, and my word's as good as my bond."

"A Shadow's word in return!" said the Shadow, for he was obliged to talk in that way. But, by the way, it was quite wonderful how complete a man he had become. He was dressed all in black, and wore the very finest black cloth, polished boots, and a hat that could be crushed together till it was nothing but crown and rim, besides what we have already noticed of him, namely, the charms, the gold neck-chain, and the diamond rings. The Shadow was indeed wonderfully well clothed; and it was just this that made a complete man of him.

"Now I will tell you," said the Shadow; and then he put down his polished boots as firmly as he could on the arm of the learned man's new shadow that lay like a poodle dog at his feet. This was done perhaps from pride, perhaps so that the new shadow might stick to his feet; but the prostrate shadow remained quite quiet, so that it might listen well, for it wanted to know how one could get free and work up to be one's own master.

"Do you know who lived in the house opposite to us?" asked the Shadow. "That was the most glorious of all; it was Poetry! I was there for three weeks, and that was just as if one had lived there a thousand years, and could read all that has been written and composed. For this I say, and it is truth, I have seen everything, and I know everything!"

"Poetry!" cried the learned man. "Yes, she often lives as a hermit in great cities. Poetry! Yes, I myself saw her for one single brief moment, but sleep was heavy on my eyes: she stood on the balcony, gleaming as the Northern Lights gleam. Tell me! tell me! You were upon the balcony. You went through the door, and then——"

"Then I was in the ante-room," said the Shadow. "You sat opposite, and were always looking across at the ante-room. There was no light; a kind of twilight reigned there; but one door after another in a whole row of halls and rooms stood open, and there it was light; and the mass of light would have killed me if I had got as far as to where the maiden sat. But I was deliberate, I took my time; and that's what one must do."

"And what didst thou see then?" asked the learned man.

"I saw everything, and I will tell you what; but—it is really not pride on my part—as a free man, and with the acquirements I possess, besides my good position and my remarkable fortune, I wish you would say *you* to me."

"I beg your pardon," said the learned man. "This *thou* is an old habit, and old habits are difficult to alter. You are perfectly right, and I will remember it. But now tell me everything you saw."

"Everything," said the Shadow; "for I saw everything, and I know everything."

"How did things look in the inner room?" asked the learned man. "Was it there as in the fresh wood? Was

it there as in a holy temple? Were the chambers like the starry sky, when one stands on the high mountains?"

"Everything was there," said the Shadow. "I was certainly not quite inside; I remained in the front room, in the darkness; but I stood there remarkably well. I saw everything and know everything. I have been in the ante-room at the Court of Poetry."

"But what did you see? Did all the gods of antiquity march through the halls? Did the old heroes fight there? Did lovely children play there, and relate their dreams?"

"I tell you that I have been there, and so you will easily understand that I saw everything that was to be seen. If *you* had got there you would not have become a man; but I became one, and at the same time I learned to understand my inner being and the relation in which I stood to Poetry. Yes, when I was with you I did not think of these things; but you know that whenever the sun rises or sets I am wonderfully great. In the moonshine I was almost more noticeable than you yourself. I did not then understand my inward being; in the ante-room it was revealed to me. I became a man! I came out ripe. But you were no longer in the warm countries. I was ashamed to go about as a man in the state I was then in: I required boots, clothes, and all this human varnish by which a man is known. I hid myself; yes, I can confide a secret to you —you will not put it into a book. I hid myself under the cake-woman's gown; the woman had no idea how much she

concealed. Only in the evening did I go out: I ran about the streets by moonlight; I stretched myself quite long up the wall: that tickled my back quite agreeably. I ran up and down, looked through the highest windows into the halls and through the roof, where nobody could see, and I saw what nobody saw and what nobody ought to see. On the whole it is a despicable world: I would not be a man if it were not commonly supposed that it is something to be one. I saw the most incredible things going on among men, and women, and parents, and 'dear incomparable children.' I saw what no one else knows, but what they all would be very glad to know, namely, bad goings on at their neighbours. If I had written a newspaper, how it would have been read! But I wrote directly to the persons interested, and there was terror in every town to which I came. They were so afraid of me that they were remarkably fond of me. The professor made me a professor; the tailor gave me new clothes (I am well provided) ; the mint-master coined money for me; the women declared I was handsome: and thus I became the man I am. And now, farewell! Here is my card; I live on the sunny side, and am always at home in rainy weather."

And the Shadow went away.

"That was very remarkable," said the learned man.

Years and days passed by, and the Shadow came again.

"How goes it?" he asked.

"Ah!" said the learned man, "I'm writing about the

true, the good, and the beautiful; but nobody cares to hear of anything of the kind: I am quite in despair, for I take that to heart."

"That I do not," said the Shadow. "I'm becoming fat and hearty, and that's what one must try to become. You don't understand the world, and you're getting ill. You must travel. I'll make a journey this summer; will you go too? I should like to have a travelling companion; will you go with me as my shadow? I shall be very happy to take you, and I'll pay the expenses."

"That's going a little too far," said the learned man.

"As you take it," replied the Shadow. "A journey will do you a great deal of good. Will you be my shadow?— then you shall have everything on the journey for nothing."

"That's too strong!" said the learned man.

"But it's the way of the world," said the Shadow, "and so it will remain!" And he went away.

The learned man was not at all fortunate. Sorrow and care pursued him, and what he said of the true and the good and the beautiful was as little valued by most people as roses would be by a cow. At last he became quite ill.

"You really look like a shadow," people said; and a shiver ran through him at these words, for he attached a peculiar meaning to them.

"You must go to a watering-place!" said the Shadow, who came to pay him a visit. "There's no other help for you? I'll take you with me, for the sake of old acquaintance.

I'll pay the expenses of the journey, and you shall make a description of it, and shorten time for me on the way. I want to visit a watering-place. My beard doesn't grow quite as it should, and that is a kind of illness; and a beard I must have. Now, be reasonable and accept my proposal: we shall travel like comrades."

And they travelled. The Shadow was master now, and the master was shadow: they drove together, they rode together, and walked side by side, and before and behind each other, just as the sun happened to stand. The shadow always knew when to take the place of honour. The learned man did not particularly notice this, for he had a very good heart, and was moreover particularly mild and friendly. Then one day the master said to the Shadow:

"As we have in this way become travelling companions, and have also from childhood's days grown up with one another, shall we not drink brotherhood? That sounds more confidential."

"You're saying a thing there," said the Shadow, who was now really the master, "that is said in a very kind and straightforward way. I will be just as kind and straightforward. You, who are a learned gentleman, know very well how wonderful nature is. There are some men who cannot bear to touch brown paper, they become sick at it; others shudder to the marrow of their bones if one scratches with a nail upon a pane of glass? and I for my part have a similar feeling when any one says 'thou' to me; I feel myself, as I did in my first position with you, oppressed by it. You see that this is a feeling, not pride. I cannot let you say 'thou' [1] to me, but I will gladly say 'thou' to you; and thus your wish will be at any rate partly fulfilled."

And now the Shadow addressed his former master as "thou."

"That's rather strong," said the latter, "that I am to say 'you,' while he says 'thou.'" But he was obliged to submit to it.

They came to a bathing-place, where many strangers were, and among them a beautiful young Princess, who had this disease, that she saw too sharply, which was very disquieting. She at once saw that the new arrival was a very different personage from all the rest.

"They say he is here to get his beard to grow; but I see the real reason—he can't throw a shadow."

She had now become inquisitive, and therefore she at once began a conversation with the strange gentleman on the promenade. As a Princess, she was not obliged to use much ceremony, therefore she said outright to him at once,

"Your illness consists in this, that you can't throw a shadow."

"Your Royal Highness must be much better," replied the Shadow. "I know your illness consists in this, that you see too sharply; but you have got the better of that. I have

---

[1] On the Continent, people who have "drunk brotherhood" address each other as "thou" in preference to the more ceremonious "you."

a very unusual shadow: don't you see the person who always accompanies me? Other people have a common shadow, but I don't love what is common. One often gives one's servants finer cloth for their liveries than one wears oneself, and so I have let my shadow deck himself out like a separate person; yes, you see I have even given him a shadow of his own. That cost very much, but I like to have something peculiar."

"How," said the Princess, "can I really have been cured? This is the best bathing-place in existence; water has wonderful power nowadays. But I'm not going away from here yet, for now it begins to be amusing. The stranger —pleases me remarkably well. I only hope his beard won't grow, for if it does he'll go away."

That evening the Princess and the Shadow danced together in the great ball-room. She was light, but he was still lighter; never had she seen such a dancer. She told him from what country she came, and he knew the country —he had been there, but just when she had been absent. He had looked through the windows of her castle, from below as well as from above; he had learned many circumstances, and could therefore make allusions, and give replies to the Princess, at which she marvelled greatly. She thought he must be the cleverest man in the world, and was inspired with great respect for all his knowledge. And when she danced with him again, she fell in love with him, and the Shadow noticed that particularly, for she looked him almost

through and through with her eyes. They danced together once more, and she was nearly telling him, but she was discreet: she thought of her country, and her kingdom, and of the many people over whom she was to rule.

"He is a clever man," she said to herself, "and that is well, and he dances capitally, and that is well too; but has he well-grounded knowledge? That is just as important, and he must be examined."

And she immediately put such a difficult question to him, that she could not have answered it herself; and the Shadow made a wry face.

"You cannot answer me that," said the Princess.

"I learned that in my childhood," replied the Shadow, "and I believe my very Shadow, standing yonder by the door, could answer it."

"Your Shadow!" cried the Princess: "that would be very remarkable."

"I do not assert as quite certain that he can do so," said the Shadow, "but I am almost inclined to believe it, he has now accompanied me and listened for so many years. But your Royal Highness will allow me to remind you that he is so proud of passing for a man, that, if he is to be in a good humour, and he should be so to answer rightly, he must be treated just like a man."

"I like that," said the Princess.

And now she went to the learned man at the door; and she spoke with him of sun and moon, of people both inside and out, and the learned man answered very cleverly and very well.

"What a man that must be, who has such a clever shadow!" she thought. "It would be a real blessing for my country and for my people if I chose him for my husband; and I'll do it!"

And they soon struck a bargain—the Princess and the Shadow; but no one was to know anything of it till she had returned to her kingdom.

"No one—not even my shadow," said the Shadow; and for this he had especial reasons.

And they came to the country where the Princess ruled, and where was her home.

"Listen, my friend," said the Shadow to the learned man. "Now I am as lucky and powerful as any one can become, I'll do something particular for you. You shall live with me in my palace, drive with me in the royal carriage, and have a hundred thousand dollars a year; but you must let yourself be called a shadow by every one, and may never say that you were once a man; and once a year, when I sit on the balcony and show myself, you must lie at my feet as it becomes my shadow to do. For I will tell you I'm going to marry the Princess, and this evening the wedding will be held."

"Now, that's too strong!" said the learned man. "I won't do it; I won't have it. That would be cheating the whole country and the Princess too. I'll tell everything—

that I'm the man and you are the Shadow, and that you are only dressed up!"

"No one would believe that," said the Shadow. "Be reasonable, or I'll call the watch."

"I'll go straight to the Princess," said the learned man.

"But I'll go first," said the Shadow; "and you shall go to prison."

And that was so; for the sentinels obeyed him who they knew was to marry the Princess.

"You tremble," said the Princess, when the Shadow came to her. "Has anything happened? You must not be ill to-day, when we are to have our wedding."

"I have experienced the most terrible thing that can happen," said the Shadow. "Only think!—such a poor shallow brain cannot bear much—only think! my shadow has gone mad: he fancies he has become a man, and—only think! —that I am his shadow."

"This is terrible!" said the Princess. "He's locked up, I hope?"

"Certainly. I'm afraid he will never recover."

"Poor shadow!" cried the Princess, "he's very unfortunate. It would really be a good action to deliver him from his little bit of life. And when I think it over properly, I believe it is quite necessary to put him quietly out of the way."

"That's certainly very hard, for he was a faithful servant," said the Shadow; and he pretended to sigh.

"You've a noble character," said the Princess, and she bowed before him.

In the evening the whole town was illuminated, and cannon were fired—bang!—and the soldiers presented arms. That *was* a wedding! The Princess and the Shadow stepped out on the balcony to show themselves and receive another cheer.

The learned man heard nothing of all this festivity, for he had already been executed.

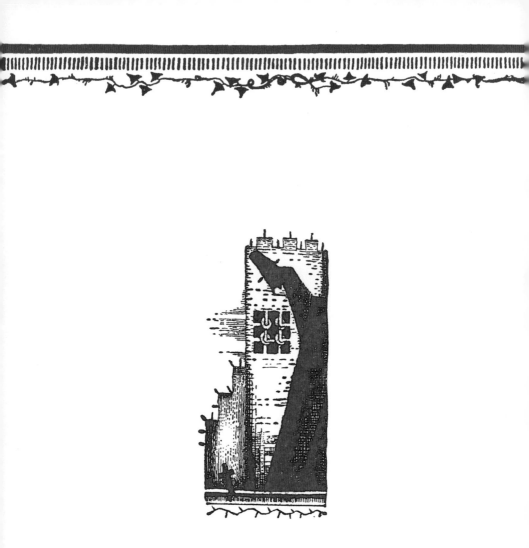

THE · SHIRT · COLLAR

THE SHIRT COLLAR

HERE was once a rich gentleman whose whole effects consisted of a Bootjack and a Hair-comb, but he had the finest Shirt Collar in the world, and about this Shirt Collar we will tell a story.

The Collar was now old enough to think of marrying, and it happened that he was sent to the wash together with a Garter.

"My word!" exclaimed the Shirt Collar. "I have never seen anything so slender and delicate, so charming and genteel. May I ask your name?"

"I shall not tell you that," said the Garter.

"Where is your home?" asked the Shirt Collar.

But the Garter was of rather a modest disposition, and it seemed such a strange question to answer.

"I presume you are a girdle?" said the Shirt Collar—"a sort of under girdle! I see that you are useful as well as ornamental, my little lady."

"You are not to speak to me," said the Garter. "I have not, I think, given you any occasion to do so."

THE SHIRT COLLAR

"Oh! when one is as beautiful as you are," cried the Shirt Collar, "that is occasion enough."

"Go!" said the Garter; "don't come so near me: you look to me quite like a man."

"I am a fine gentleman, too," said the Shirt Collar. "I possess a bootjack and a hair-comb."

And that was not true at all, for it was his master who owned these things, but he was boasting.

"Don't come too near me," said the Garter; "I'm not used to that."

"Affectation!" cried the Shirt Collar.

And then they were taken out of the wash, and starched, and hung over a chair in the sunshine, and then laid on the ironing-board; and now came the hot Iron.

"Mrs. Widow!" said the Shirt Collar, "little Mrs. Widow, I'm getting quite warm; I'm being quite changed; I'm losing all my creases; you're burning a hole in me! Ugh! I propose to you."

"You old rag!" said the Iron, and rode proudly over the Shirt Collar, for it imagined that it was a steam boiler, and that it ought to be out on the railway, dragging carriages. "You old rag!" said the Iron.

The Shirt Collar was a little frayed at the edges, therefore the Paper Scissors came to smooth away the frayed places.

"Ho, ho!" said the Shirt Collar; "I presume you are a

first-rate dancer. How you can point your toes! no one in the world can do that like you."

"I know that," said the Scissors.

"You deserve to be a countess," said the Shirt Collar. "All that I possess consists of a fine gentleman, a bootjack, and a comb. If I had only an estate!"

"What! do you want to marry?" cried the Scissors; and they were angry, and gave such a deep cut that the Collar had to be cashiered.

"I shall have to propose to the Hair-comb," thought the Shirt Collar. "It is wonderful how well you keep all your teeth, my little lady. Have you never thought of engaging yourself?"

"Yes, you can easily imagine that," replied the Hair-comb. "I am engaged to the Bootjack."

"Engaged!" cried the Shirt Collar.

Now there was no one left to whom he could offer himself, and so he despised love-making.

A long time passed, and the Shirt Collar was put into the sack of a paper-miller. There was a terribly ragged company, and the fine ones kept to themselves, and the coarse ones to themselves, as is right. They all had much to tell, but the Shirt Collar had most of all, for he was a terrible Jack Brag.

"I have had a tremendous number of sweethearts," said the Shirt Collar. "They would not leave me alone; but I

THE SHIRT COLLAR

was a fine gentleman, a starched one. I had a bootjack and a hair-comb that I never used: you should only have seen me then, when I was turned down. I shall never forget my first love; it was a girdle; and how delicate, how charming, how genteel it was! And my first love threw herself into a washing-tub, and all for me! There was also a widow who became quite glowing, but I let her stand alone till she turned quite black. Then there was a dancer who gave me the wound from which I still suffer—she was very hot-tempered. My own hair-comb was in love with me, and lost all her teeth from neglected love. Yes, I've had many experiences of this kind; but I am most sorry for the Garter—I mean for the girdle, that jumped into the wash-tub for love of me. I've a great deal on my conscience. It's time I was turned into white paper."

And to that the Shirt Collar came. All the rags were turned into white paper, but the Shirt Collar became the very piece of paper we see here, and upon which this story has been printed, and that was done because he boasted so dreadfully about things that were not at all true. And this we must remember, so that we may on no account do the same, for we cannot know at all whether we shall not be put into the rag bag and manufactured into white paper, on which our whole history, even the most secret, shall be printed, so that we shall be obliged to run about and tell it, as the Shirt Collar did.

THE · BOTTLE · NECK

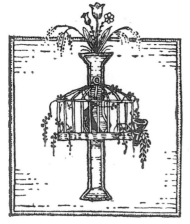

N a narrow crooked street, among other abodes of poverty, stood an especially narrow and tall house built of timber, which had given way in every direction. The house was inhabited by poor people, and the deepest poverty was in the garret-lodging in the gable, where, in front of the only window, hung an old bent birdcage, which had not even a proper water-glass, but only a Bottle-neck reversed, with a cork stuck in the mouth, and filled with water. An old maid stood by the window: she had hung the cage with green chickweed; and a little chaffinch hopped from perch to perch, and sang and twittered merrily enough.

"Yes, it's all very well for you to sing," said the Bottle-neck; that is to say, it did not pronounce the words as we can speak them, for a bottle-neck can't speak; but that's what he thought to himself in his own mind, as when we people talk quietly to ourselves. "Yes, it's all very well for you to sing, you that have all your limbs uninjured. You ought to feel what it's like to lose one's body, and to have only mouth and neck left, and that with a cork

into the bargain, as in my case; and then I'm sure you would not sing. But after all it is well that there should be somebody at least who is merry. I've no reason to sing, and, moreover, I can't sing. Yes, when I was a whole bottle, I sang out well if they rubbed me with a cork. They used to call me a perfect lark, a magnificent lark! Ah, when I was out at a picnic with the tanner's family, and his daughter was betrothed! Yes, I remember it as if it had happened only yesterday. I have gone through a great deal, when I come to recollect. I've been in the fire and the water, have been deep in the black earth, and have mounted higher than most of the others; and now I'm hanging here, outside the birdcage, in the air and the sunshine! Oh, it would be quite worth while to hear my history; but I don't speak aloud of it because I can't."

And now the Bottle-neck told its story, which was sufficiently remarkable. It told the story to itself, or only thought it in its own mind; and the little bird sang his song merrily, and down in the street there was driving and hurrying, and every one thought of his own affairs, or perhaps of nothing at all; but the Bottle-neck did think. It thought of a flaming furnace in the manufactory, where it had blown into life; it still remembered that it had been quite warm, that it had glanced into the hissing furnace, the home of its origin, and had felt a great desire to leap directly back again; but that gradually it had become cooler, and had been very comfortable in the place to which it was taken. It had stood in a rank with a whole regiment of brothers and sisters, all out of the same furnace; some of them had certainly been blown into champagne bottles, and others into beer bottles, and that makes a difference. Later, out in the world, it may well happen that a beer bottle may contain the most precious wine, and a champagne bottle be filled with blacking; but even in decay there is always something left by which people can see what one has been —nobility is nobility, even when filled with blacking.

All the bottles were packed up, and our bottle was among them. At the time it did not think to finish its career as a bottle-neck, or that it should work its way up to be a bird's glass, which is always an honourable thing, for one is of some consequence, after all. The bottle did not again behold the light of day till it was unpacked with the other bottles in the cellar of the wine merchant and rinsed out for the first time; and that was a strange sensation. There it lay, empty and without a cork, and felt strangely unwell, as if it wanted something, it could not tell what. At last it was filled with good costly wine, and was provided with a cork, and sealed down. A ticket was placed on it marked "first quality"; and it felt as if it had carried off first prize at an examination; for, you see, the wine was good and the bottle was good. When one is young, that's the time for poetry! There was a singing and sounding within it, of things which it could not understand—of green sunny mountains, whereon the grape grows, where many vine dressers.

men and women, sing and dance and rejoice. "Ah, how beautiful is life!" There was a singing and sounding of all this in the bottle, as in a young poet's brain; and many a young poet does not understand the meaning of the song that is within him.

One morning the bottle was bought, for the tanner's apprentice was dispatched for a bottle of wine—"of the best." And now it was put in the provision basket, with ham and cheese and sausages; the finest butter and the best bread were put into the basket too—the tanner's daughter herself packed it. She was young and very pretty; her brown eyes laughed, and round her mouth played a smile which said just as much as her eyes. She had delicate hands, beautifully white, and her neck was whiter still; you saw at once that she was one of the most beautiful girls in the town: and still she was not engaged.

The provision basket was in the lap of the young girl when the family drove out into the forest. The Bottle-neck looked out from the folds of the white napkin. There was red wax upon the cork, and the bottle looked straight into the girl's face. It also looked at the young sailor who sat next to the girl. He was a friend of old days, the son of the portrait painter. Quite lately he had passed with honour through his examination as mate, and to-morrow he was to sail away in a ship, far off to a distant land. There had been much talk of this while the basket was being packed;

and certainly the eyes and mouth of the tanner's pretty daughter did not wear a very joyous expression just then.

The young people sauntered through the greenwood, and talked to one another. What were they talking of? No, the bottle could not hear that, for it was in the provision basket. A long time passed before it was drawn forth; but when that happened, there had been pleasant things going on, for all were laughing, and the tanner's daughter laughed too; but she spoke less than before, and her cheeks glowed like two roses.

The father took the full bottle and the corkscrew in his hand. Yes, it's a strange thing to be drawn thus, the first time! The Bottle-neck could never afterwards forget that impressive moment; and indeed, there was quite a convulsion within him when the cork flew out, and a great throbbing as the wine poured forth into the glasses.

"Health to the betrothed pair!" cried the papa. And every glass was emptied to the bottom, and the young mate kissed his beautiful bride.

"Happiness and blessing!" said the two old people. And the young man filled the glasses again.

"Safe return, and a wedding this day next year!" he cried; and when the glasses were emptied, he took the bottle, raised it on high, and said, "Thou hast been present at the happiest day of my life, thou shalt never serve another!"

And so saying, he hurled it high into the air. The

tanner's daughter did not then think that she should see the bottle fly again; and yet it was to be so. It then fell into the thick reeds on the margin of a little woodland lake; and the Bottle-neck could remember quite plainly how it lay there for some time.

"I gave them wine, and they give me marsh water," he said, "but it is well meant."

He could no longer see the betrothed couple and the cheerful old people; but for a long time he could hear them rejoicing and singing; then at last came two peasant boys, and looked into the reeds; they spied out the bottle, and took it up; and now it was provided for.

At their home, in the wooden cottage, the eldest of three brothers, who was a sailor, and about to start on a long voyage, had been the day before to take leave. The mother was just engaged in packing up various things he was to take with him upon his journey, and which the father was going to carry into the town that evening to see his son once more, to give him a farewell greeting from the lad's mother and himself, and a little bottle of medicated brandy had already been wrapped up in a parcel, when the boys came in with the larger and stronger bottle which they had found. This bottle would hold more than the little one, and they pronounced that the brandy would be capital for a bad digestion, inasmuch as it was mixed with medical herbs. The draught that was poured into the bottle was not so good as the red wine with which it had once been filled;

these were bitter thoughts, but even these are sometimes good. The new big bottle was to go, and not the little one; and so the bottle went travelling again. It was taken on board for Peter Jensen, in the very same ship in which the young mate sailed. But he did not see the bottle; and, indeed, he would not have known it, or thought it was the same one out of which had been drunk a health to the betrothed pair and to his own happy return.

Certainly it had no longer wine to give, but still it contained something that was just as good. Accordingly, whenever Peter Jensen brought it out, it was dubbed by his messmates The Apothecary. It contained the best medicine, medicine that strengthened the weak, and it gave liberally so long as it had a drop left. That was a pleasant time, and the bottle sang when it was rubbed with the cork; and it was called the Great Lark, "Peter Jensen's Lark."

Long days and months rolled on, and the bottle already stood empty in a corner, when it happened—whether on the passage out or home the bottle could not tell, for it had never been ashore—that a storm arose; great waves came careering along, darkly and heavily, and lifted and tossed the ship to and fro. The mainmast was shivered, and a wave started one of the planks, and the pumps became useless. It was black night. The ship sank; but at the last moment the young mate wrote on a leaf of paper, "God's will be done! We are sinking!" He wrote the name of his betrothed, and his own name, and that of the ship, and put the leaf in an empty bottle that happened to be at hand: he corked it firmly down and threw it out into the foaming sea. He knew not that it was the very bottle from which the goblet of joy and hope had once been filled for him and for her; and now it was tossing on the waves with his last greeting and the message of death.

The ship sank, and the crew sank with her. The bottle sped on like a bird, for it bore a heart, a loving letter, within itself. And the sun rose and set; and the bottle felt as at the time when it first came into being in the red gleaming oven—it felt a strong desire to leap back into the light.

It experienced calms and fresh storms; but it was hurled against no rock, and was devoured by no shark; and thus it drifted on for a year and a day, sometimes towards the north, sometimes towards the south, just as the current carried it. Beyond this it was its own master, but one may grow tired even of that.

The written page, the last farewell of a sweetheart to his betrothed, would only bring sorrow if it came into her hands; but where were the hands, so white and delicate, which had once spread the cloth on the fresh grass in the greenwood, on the betrothal day? Where was the tanner's daughter? Yes, where was the land, and which land might be nearest to her dwelling? The bottle knew not; it drove onward and onward, and was at last tired of wandering because that was not in its way; but yet it had to travel until at last it came to land—to a strange land. It under-

stood not a word of what was spoken here, for this was not the language it had heard spoken before; and one loses a good deal if one does not understand the language.

The bottle was fished out and examined. The leaf of paper within it was discovered, and taken out, and turned over and over but the people did not understand what was written thereon. They saw that the bottle must have been thrown overboard, and that something about this was written on the paper, but what were the words? That question remained unanswered, and the paper was put back into the bottle, and the latter was deposited in a great cupboard in a great room in a great house.

Whenever strangers came the paper was brought out and turned over and over, so that the inscription, which was only written in pencil, became more and more illegible, so that at last no one could see that there were letters on it. And for a whole year more the bottle remained standing in the cupboard; and then it was put into the loft, where it became covered with dust and cobwebs. Then it thought of the better days, the times when it had poured forth red wine in the greenwood, when it had been rocked on the waves of the sea, and when it had carried a secret, a letter, a parting sigh.

For full twenty years it stood up in the loft; and it might have remained there longer, but that the house was to be rebuilt. The roof was taken off, and then the bottle was noticed, and they spoke about it, but it did not understand their language; for one cannot learn a language by being shut up in a loft, even if one stays there twenty years.

"If I had been down in the room," thought the Bottle, "I might have learned it."

It was now washed and rinsed, and indeed this was requisite. It felt quite transparent and fresh, and as if its youth had been renewed in this its old age; but the paper it had carried so faithfully had been destroyed in the washing.

The bottle was filled with seeds, it did not know the kind. It was corked and well wrapped up. It saw neither lantern nor candle, to say nothing of sun or moon; and yet it thought, when one goes on a journey one ought to see something; but though it saw nothing, it did what was most important—it travelled to the place of its destination, and was there unpacked.

"What trouble they have taken over yonder with that bottle!" it heard people say; "and yet it is most likely broken." But it was not broken.

The bottle understood every word that was now said; this was the language it had heard at the furnace, and at the wine merchant's, and in the forest, and in the ship, the only good old language it understood: it had come back home, and the language was as a salutation of welcome to it. For very joy it felt ready to jump out of people's hands; hardly did it notice that its cork had been drawn, and that it had been emptied and carried into the cellar, to be placed

there and forgotten. There is no place like home, even if it's in a cellar! It never occurred to the bottle to think how long it lay there, for it felt comfortable, and accordingly lay there for years. At last people came down into the cellar to carry off all the bottles, and ours amongst the rest.

Out in the garden there was a great festival. Flaming lamps hung like garlands, and paper lanterns shone transparent, like great tulips. The evening was lovely, the weather still and clear, the stars twinkled; it was the time of the new moon, but in reality the whole moon could be seen as a bluish-grey disc with a golden rim round half its surface, which was a very beautiful sight for those who had good eyes.

The illumination extended even to the most retired of the garden walks; at least, so much of it that one could find one's way there. Among the leaves of the hedges stood bottles, with a light in each; and among them was also the bottle we know, and which was destined one day to finish its career as a bottle-neck, a bird's drinking-glass. Everything here appeared lovely to our bottle, for it was once more in the greenwood, amid joy and feasting, and heard song and music, and the noise and murmur of a crowd, especially in that part of the garden where the lamps blazed and the paper lanterns displayed their many colours. Thus it stood, in a distant walk certainly, but that made it the more important; for it bore its light, and was at once ornamental and useful, and that is as it should be: in such an hour one forgets twenty years spent in a loft, and it is right one should do so.

There passed close to it a pair, like a pair who had walked together long ago in the wood, the sailor and the tanner's daughter; the bottle seemed to experience all that over again. In the garden were walking not only the guests, but other people who were allowed to view all the splendour; and among these latter came an old maid without kindred, but not without friends. She was just thinking, like the bottle, of the greenwood, and of a young betrothed pair—of a pair which concerned her very nearly, a pair in which she had an interest, and of which she had been a part in that happiest hour of her life—the hour one never forgets, if one should become ever so old a maid. But she did not know the bottle, and it did not know her: it is thus we pass each other in the world, meeting again and again, as these two met, now that they were together again in the same town.

From the garden the bottle was despatched once more to the wine merchant's, where it was filled with wine and sold to the aeronaut, who was to make an ascent in his balloon on the following Sunday. A great crowd had assembled to witness the sight; military music had been provided, and many other preparations had been made. The bottle saw everything from a basket in which it lay next to a live rabbit, which latter was quite bewildered because he

knew he was to be taken up into the air, and let down again in a parachute; but the bottle knew nothing of the "up" or the "down"; it only saw the balloon swelling up bigger and bigger, and at last, when it could swell no more, beginning to rise, and to grow more and more restless. The ropes that held it were cut, and the huge machine floated aloft with the aeronaut and the basket containing the bottle and the rabbit, and the music sounded, and all the people cried, "Hurrah!"

"This is a wonderful passage, up into the air!" thought the Bottle; "this is a new way of sailing; at any rate, up here we cannot strike upon anything."

Thousands of people gazed up at the balloon, and the old maid looked up at it also; she stood at the open window of the garret, in which hung the cage, with the little chaffinch, who had no water-glass as yet, but was obliged to be content with an old cup.

In the window stood a myrtle in a pot; and it had been put a little aside that it might not fall out, for the old maid was leaning out of the window to look, and she distinctly saw the aeronaut in the balloon, and how he let down the rabbit in the parachute, and then drank the health of all the spectators, and at length hurled the bottle high in the air; she never thought that this was the identical bottle which she had already once seen thrown aloft in honour of her and of her friend on the day of rejoicing in the greenwood, in the time of her youth.

THE BOTTLE-NECK

The bottle had no time for thought, for it was quite startled at thus suddenly reaching the highest point in its career. Steeples and roofs lay far, far beneath, and the people looked like mites.

But now it began to descend with a much more rapid fall than that of the rabbit; the bottle threw somersaults in the air, and felt quite young, and quite free and unfettered; and yet it was half full of wine, though it did not remain so for long. What a journey! The sun shone on the bottle, all the people were looking at it; the balloon was already far away, and soon the bottle was far away too, for it fell upon a roof and broke; but the pieces had got such an impetus that they could not stop themselves, but went jumping and rolling on till they came down into the courtyard and lay there in smaller pieces yet; only the Bottle-neck managed to keep whole, and that was cut off as if it had been done with a diamond.

"That would do capitally for a bird-glass," said the cellar-man; but he had neither a bird nor a cage; and to expect him to provide both because they had found a bottle-neck that might be available for a glass, would have been expecting too much; but the old maid in the garret, perhaps it might be useful to her; and now the Bottle-neck was taken up to her, and was provided with a cork. The part that had been uppermost was now turned downwards, as often happens when changes take place; fresh water was poured

into it, and it was fastened to the cage of the little bird, which sang and twittered right merrily.

"Yes, it's very well for you to sing," said the Bottle-neck.

And it was considered remarkable for having been in the balloon—for that was all they knew of its history. Now it hung there as a bird-glass, and heard the murmuring and noise of the people in the street below, and also the words of the old maid in the room within. An old friend had just come to visit her, and they talked—not of the Bottle-neck, but about the myrtle in the window.

"No, you certainly must not spend two dollars for your daughter's bridal wreath," said the old maid. "You shall have a beautiful little nosegay from me, full of blossoms. Do you see how splendidly that tree has come on? yes, that has been raised from a spray of the myrtle you gave me on the day after my betrothal, and from which I was to have made my own wreath when the year was past; but that day never came! The eyes closed that were to have been my joy and delight through life. In the depths of the sea he sleeps sweetly, my dear one! The myrtle had become an old tree, and I have become a yet older woman; and when it faded at last, I took the last green shoot, and planted it in the ground, and it has become a great tree; and now at length the myrtle will serve at the wedding—as a wreath for your daughter."

THE BOTTLE-NECK

There were tears in the eyes of the old maid. She spoke of the beloved of her youth, of their betrothal in the wood; many thoughts came to her, but the thought never came that, quite close to her, before the very window, was a remembrance of those times—the neck of the bottle which had shouted for joy when the cork had flown out with a bang on the betrothal day. But the Bottle-neck did not recognise her either, for he was not listening to what she said—partly because it only thought about itself.

THE · ELDER · TREE · MOTHER

THE ELDER TREE MOTHER

HERE was once a little boy who had caught cold; he had gone out and got wet feet; no one could imagine how it had happened, for it was quite dry weather. Now his mother undressed him, put him to bed, and had the tea-urn brought in to make him a good cup of elder tea, for that warms well. At the same time there also came in at the door the friendly old man who lived all alone at the top of the house, and was very solitary. He had neither wife nor children, but he was very fond of all children and knew so many stories that it was quite delightful.

"Now you are to drink your tea," said the mother, "and then perhaps you will hear a story."

"Ah! if one only could tell a new one!" said the old man, with a friendly nod. "But where did the little man get his feet wet?" he asked.

"Yes," replied the mother, "no one can imagine how that came about."

"Shall I have a story?" asked the boy.

"Yes, if you can tell me at all accurately—for I must

know that first—how deep the gutter is in the little street through which you go to school."

"Just half-way up to my knee," answered the boy, "that is, if I put my feet in the deep hole."

"You see, that's how we get our feet wet," said the old gentleman. "Now I ought certainly to tell you a story; but I don't know any more."

"You can make up one directly," answered the little boy. "Mother says that everything you look at can be turned into a story, and that you can make a tale of everything you touch."

"Yes, but those stories and tales are worth nothing! No, the real ones come of themselves. They knock at my forehead, and say, 'Here I am!'"

"Will there soon be a knock?" asked the little boy, and the mother laughed, and put elder tea in the pot, and poured hot water upon it.

"A story! a story!"

"Yes, if a story would come of itself; but that kind of thing is very grand; it only comes when it's in the humour. —Wait!" he cried all at once; "here we have it. Look you; there's one in the tea-pot now."

And the little boy looked across at the tea-pot. The lid raised itself more and more, and the elder flowers came forth from it, white and fresh; they shot forth long fresh branches even out of the spout, they spread abroad in all directions,

244

And in the midst of the tree sat an old,
pleasant-looking woman in a strange
dress.

[See Page 247]

and became larger and larger; there was the most glorious elder bush—in fact, quite a great tree. It penetrated even to the bed, and thrust the curtains aside; how fragrant it was, and how it bloomed! And in the midst of the tree sat an old, pleasant-looking woman in a strange dress. It was quite green, like the leaves of the elder tree, and bordered with great white elder blossoms; one could not at once discern whether this border was of stuff or of living green and real flowers.

"What is the woman's name?" the little boy asked.

"The Romans and Greeks," replied the old man, "used to call her a Dryad; but we don't understand that: out in the sailors' quarter we have a better name for her; there she's called Elder Tree Mother, and it is to her you must pay attention; only listen, and look at that glorious elder tree.

"Just such a great blooming tree stands out in the sailors' quarter; it grew there in the corner of a poor little yard, and under this tree two old people sat one afternoon in the brightest sunshine. It was an old, old sailor, and his old, old wife; they had great-grandchildren, and were soon to celebrate their golden wedding; but they could not quite make out the date, and the Elder Tree Mother sat in the tree and looked pleased, just as she does here. 'I know very well when the golden wedding is to be,' said she; but they did not hear it—they were talking of old times.

" 'Yes, do you remember,' said the old seaman, 'when

we were quite little, and ran about and played together! It was in the very same yard where we are sitting now, and we planted little twigs in the yard, and made a garden.'

" 'Yes,' replied the old woman, 'I remember it very well: we watered the twigs, and one of them was an elder twig; that struck root, shot out other green twigs, and has become the great tree, under which we old people sit.'

" 'Surely,' said he; 'and yonder in the corner stood a butt of water; there I swam my boat; I had cut it out myself. How it could sail! But I certainly soon had to sail in a different fashion myself.'

" 'But first we went to school and learned something,' said she, 'and then we were confirmed; we both cried, but in the afternoon we went hand in hand to the round tower, and looked out into the wide world, over Copenhagen and across the water; then we went out to Fredericksberg, where the King and Queen were sailing in their splendid boats upon the canals.'

" 'But I was obliged to sail in another fashion, and that for many years, far away on long voyages.'

" 'Yes, I often cried about you,' she said. 'I thought you were dead and gone, and lying down in the deep waters, rocked by the waves. Many a night I got up to look if the weathercock was turning. Yes, it turned indeed; but you did not come. I remember so clearly how the rain streamed down one day. The man with the cart who fetched away the dust came to the place where I was in service. I went down to him with the dust-bin, and remained standing in the doorway. What wretched weather it was! And just as I stood there the postman came up and gave me a letter. It was from you! How that letter had travelled about! I tore it open and read; I laughed and wept at once, I was so glad. There it stood written that you were in the warm countries where the coffee-beans grow. What a delightful land that must be! You told me so much, and I read it all while the rain was streaming down, and I stood by the dust-bin. Then somebody came and clasped me round the waist.'

" 'And you gave him a terrible box on the ear—one that sounded?'

" 'I did not know that it was you. You had arrived just as quickly as your letter. And you were so handsome; but that you are still. You had a long yellow silk handkerchief in your pocket, and a shiny hat on your head. You were so handsome! And gracious! what weather it was, and how the street looked!'

" 'Then we were married,' said he; 'do you remember? And then when our first little boy came, and then Marie, and Neils, and Peter and Hans Christian?'

" 'Yes, and how all of these have grown up to be respectable people, and every one likes them.'

" 'And their children have had little ones in their turn,' said the old sailor. " 'Yes, those are children's children! They're of the right sort. It was, if I don't mistake, at this very season of the year that we were married?'

249

THE ELDER TREE MOTHER

" 'Yes; this is the day of your golden wedding,' said the Elder Tree Mother, putting out her head just between the two old people; and they thought it was a neighbour nodding to them, and they looked at each other, and took hold of one another's hands.

"Soon afterwards came their children and grandchildren; these knew very well that it was the golden wedding-day; they had already brought their congratulations in the morning, but the old people had forgotten it, while they remembered everything right well that had happened years and years ago.

"And the elder tree smelt so strong, and the sun that was just setting shone just in the faces of the old people, so that their cheeks looked quite red; and the youngest of their grandchildren danced about them, and cried out quite gleefully that there was to be a feast this evening, for they were to have hot potatoes; and the Elder Mother nodded in the tree, and called out 'hurrah!' with all the rest."

"But that was not a story," said the little boy who had heard it told.

"Yes, if you could understand it," replied the old man; "but let us ask the Elder Mother about it."

"That was not a story," said the Elder Mother; "but now it comes; but of truth the strangest stories are formed, otherwise my beautiful elder tree could not have sprouted forth out of the tea-pot."

And then she took the little boy out of bed, and laid

him upon her bosom, and the blossoming elder branches wound round them, so that they sat as it were in the thickest arbour, and this arbour flew with them through the air. It was indescribably beautiful. Elder Mother all at once became a pretty young girl; but her dress was still of the green stuff with the white blossoms that Elder Mother had worn; in her bosom she had a real elder blossom, and about her yellow curly hair a wreath of elder flowers; her eyes were so large and blue, they were beautiful to look at. She and the boy were of the same age, and they kissed each other and felt similar joys.

Hand in hand they went forth out of the arbour, and now they stood in the beauteous flower garden of home. The father's staff was tied up near the fresh grass-plot, and for the little boy there was life in that staff. As soon as they seated themselves upon it, the polished head turned into a noble neighing horse's head, with a flowing mane, and four slender legs shot forth; the creature was strong and spirited, and they rode at a gallop round the grass-plot— hurrah!

"Now we're going to ride many miles away," said the boy; "we'll ride to the nobleman's estate, where we went last year!"

And they rode round and round the grass-plot, and the little girl, who, as we know, was no one else but Elder Mother, kept crying out,

"Now we're in the country! Do you see the farmhouse,

with the great baking-oven standing out of the wall like an enormous egg by the wayside? The elder tree spreads its branches over it, and the cock walks about, scratching for his hens; look how he struts! Now we are near the church; it lies high up on the hill, among the great oak trees, one of which is half dead. Now we are at the forge, where the fire burns and the half-clad men beat with their hammers, so that the sparks fly far around. Away, away to the nobleman's splendid seat!"

And everything that the little maiden mentioned, as she sat on the stick behind him, flew past them, and the little boy saw it all, though they were only riding round and round the grass-plot. Then they played in the side-walk, and scratched up the earth to make a little garden; and she took elder flowers out of her hair and planted them, and they grew just like those that the old people had planted when they were little, as has been already told. They went hand in hand just as the old people had done in their childhood; but not to the round tower, or to the Fredericksberg Garden. No, the little girl took hold of the boy round the body, and then they flew here and there over the whole of Denmark.

And it was spring, and summer came, and autumn, and winter, and thousands of pictures were mirrored in the boy's eyes and heart, and the little maiden was always singing to him.

He will never forget that; and throughout their whole

journey the elder tree smelt so sweet, so fragrant; he noticed the roses and the fresh beech trees; but the elder tree smelt stronger than all, for its flowers hung round the little girl's heart, and he often leaned against them as they flew onward.

"How beautiful it is here in spring!" said the little girl.

And they stood in the new-leaved beech wood, where the green woodruff lay spread in fragrance at their feet, and the pale pink anemones looked glorious among the vivid green.

"Oh, that it were always spring in the fragrant Danish beech woods!"

"How beautiful it is here in summer!" said she.

And they passed by old castles of knightly days, castles whose red walls and pointed gables were mirrored in the canals, where swans swam about, and looked down the old shady avenues. In the fields the corn waved like a sea, in the ditches yellow and red flowers were growing, and in the hedges wild hops and blooming convolvulus. In the evening the moon rose round and large, and the haystacks in the meadows smelt sweet.

"How beautiful it is here in autumn!" said the little girl.

And the sky seemed twice as lofty and twice as blue as before, and the forest was decked in the most gorgeous tints of red, yellow, and green. The hunting dogs raced about; whole flocks of wild ducks flew screaming over the ancient

grave-mound, on which bramble bushes twined over the old stones. The sea was dark blue, and covered with ships and white sails; and in the barns sat old women, girls, and children, picking hops into a large tub: the young people sang songs, and the older ones told tales of magicians and goblins. It could not be finer anywhere.

"How beautiful it is here in winter!" said the little girl.

And all the trees were covered with hoar frost, so that they looked like white trees of coral. The snow crackled beneath one's feet, as if every one had new boots on; and one shooting star after another fell from the sky. In the room the Christmas tree was lighted up, and there were presents, and there was happiness. In the country people's farmhouses the violin sounded, and there were merry games for apples; and even the poorest child said, "It is beautiful in winter!"

Yes, it was beautiful; and the little girl showed the boy everything; and still the blossoming tree smelt sweet, and still waved the red flag with the white cross, the flag under which the old seaman had sailed. The boy became a youth, and was to go out into the wide world, far away to the hot countries where the coffee grows. But when they were to part the little girl took an elder blossom from her breast, and gave it to him to keep. It was laid in his hymn-book, and in the foreign land, when he opened the book, it was always at the place where the flower of remembrance lay; and the more he looked at the flower the fresher it became, so that he seemed, as it were, to breathe the forest air of home; then he plainly saw the little girl looking out with her clear blue eyes from between the petals of the flower, and then she whispered, "How beautiful it is here in spring, summer, autumn, and winter!" and hundreds of pictures glided through his thoughts.

Thus many years went by, and now he was an old man, and sat with his old wife under the blossoming elder tree: they were holding each other by the hand, just as the great-grandmother and great-grandfather had done before; and, like these, they spoke of old times and of the golden wedding. The little maiden with the blue eyes and with the elder blossoms in her hair sat up in the tree, and nodded to both of them, and said, "To-day is the golden wedding-day!" and then she took two flowers out of her hair and kissed them, and they gleamed first like silver and then like gold, and when she laid them on the heads of the old people each changed into a golden crown. There they both sat, like a King and a Queen, under the fragrant tree which looked quite like an elder bush, and he told his old wife of the story of the Elder Tree Mother, as it had been told to him when he was quite a little boy, and they both thought that there was so much in the story that resembled their own, and those parts they liked the best.

"Yes, thus it is!" said the little girl in the tree. "Some call me Elder Tree Mother, others the Dryad, but my real name is Remembrance: it is I who sit in the tree that grows

on and on, and I can think back and tell stories. Let me see if you have still your flower."

And the old man opened his hymn-book; there lay the elder blossom as fresh as if it had only just been placed there; and Remembrance nodded, and the two old people with the golden crowns on their heads sat in the red evening sunlight, and they closed their eyes, and—and—the story was finished.

The little boy lay in his bed and did not know whether he had been dreaming or had heard a tale told; the tea-pot stood on the table, but no elder bush was growing out of it, and the old man who had told about it was just going out of the door, and indeed he went.

"How beautiful that was!" said the little boy. "Mother, I have been in the hot countries."

"Yes, I can imagine that!" replied his mother. "When one drinks two cups of hot elder tea one very often gets into the hot countries!" And she covered him up well, that he might not take cold. "You have slept well while I disputed with him as to whether it was a story or a fairy tale."

"And where is the Elder Tree Mother?" asked the little lad.

"She's in the teapot," replied his mother; "and there she may stay."

THE · STORY · OF · A · MOTHER

THE STORY OF A MOTHER

MOTHER sat by her little child: she was very sorrowful, fearing that it would die. Its little face was pale, and its eyes were closed. The child drew its breath with difficulty, and sometimes as deeply as if it were sighing; and then the mother looked more sorrowfully than before on the little creature.

There was a knock at the door, and a poor old man came in, wrapped up in something that looked like a great horse-cloth, for that keeps one warm; and he needed it, for it was cold winter. Without, everything was covered with ice and snow, and the wild wind blew so sharply that it cut one's face.

And as the old man trembled with cold, and the child was quiet for a moment, the mother went and put some beer on the stove in a little pot, to warm it for him. The old man sat down and rocked the cradle, and the mother seated herself on a chair by him, looked at her sick child that drew its breath so painfully, and lifted the little child.

"You think I shall keep it, do you not?" she asked. "The good God will not take it from me!"

THE STORY OF A MOTHER

And the old man—he was *Death*—nodded in such a strange way, that it might just as well mean *yes* as *no*. And the mother cast down her eyes, and tears rolled down her cheeks. Her head became heavy: for three days and three nights she had not closed her eyes; and now she slept, but only for a minute; then she started up and shivered with cold.

"What is that?" she asked, and looked round on all sides; but the old man was gone, and her little child was gone; he had taken it with him. And there in the corner the old clock was humming and whirring; the heavy leaden weight ran down to the floor—plump!—and the clock stopped.

But the poor mother rushed out of the house crying for her child.

Out in the snow sat a woman in long black garments, and she said, "Death has been with you in your room; I saw him hasten away with your child: he strides faster than the wind, and never brings back what he has taken away."

"Only tell me which way he has gone," said the mother. "Tell me the way, and I will find him."

"I know him," said the woman in the black garments; "but before I tell you, you must sing me all the songs that you have sung to your child. I love those songs; I have heard them before. I am Night, and I saw your tears when you sang them."

"I will sing them all, all!" said the mother. "But do not detain me, that I may overtake him, and find my child."

But Night sat dumb and still. Then the mother wrung her hands, and sang and wept. And there were many songs, but yet more tears, and then Night said, "Go to the right into the dark fir wood; for I saw Death take that path with your little child."

Deep into the forest there was a cross-road, and she did not know which way to take. There stood a thorn bush, with not a leaf nor a blossom upon it; for it was in the cold winter-time, and icicles hung from the twigs.

"Have you not seen Death go by, with my little child?"

"Yes," replied the Bush, "but I shall not tell you which way he went unless you warm me in your bosom. I'm freezing to death here, I'm turning to ice."

And she pressed the thorn bush to her bosom, quite close, that it might be well warmed. And the thorns pierced into her flesh, and her blood oozed out in great drops. But the thorn shot out fresh green leaves, and blossomed in the dark winter night: so warm is the heart of a sorrowing mother! And the thorn bush told her the way that she should go.

Then she came to a great lake, on which there were neither ships nor boat. The lake was not frozen enough to carry her, nor sufficiently open to allow her to wade through, and yet she must cross if she was to find her child. Then she laid herself down to drink the lake; and that was impossible for any one to do. But the sorrowing mother thought that perhaps a miracle might be wrought.

"No, that can never succeed," said the lake. "Let us rather see how we can agree. I'm fond of collecting pearls, and your eyes are the two clearest I have ever seen: if you will weep them out into me I will carry you over into the great greenhouse, where Death lives and cultivates flowers and trees; each of these is a human life."

"Oh, what would I not give to get my child!" said the afflicted mother; and she wept yet more, and her eyes fell into the depths of the lake, and became two costly pearls. But the lake lifted her up, as if she sat in a swing, and wafted her to the opposite shore, where stood a wonderful house, miles in length. One could not tell if it was a mountain containing forests and caves, or a place that had been built. But the poor mother could not see it, for she had wept her eyes out.

"Where shall I find Death, who went away with my little child?" she asked.

"He has not arrived here yet," said the old grave-woman, who was going about and watching the hothouse of Death. "How have you found your way here, and who helped you?"

"The good God has helped me," she replied. "He is merciful, and you will be merciful too. Where shall I find my little child?"

"I do not know it," said the old woman, "and you cannot see. Many flowers and trees have faded this night, and

Death will soon come and transplant them. You know very well that every human being has his tree of life, or his flower of life, just as each is arranged. They look like other plants, but their hearts beat. Children's hearts can beat too. Go by that. Perhaps you may recognise the beating of your child's heart. But what will you give me if I tell you what more you must do?"

"I have nothing more to give," said the afflicted mother. "But I will go for you to the ends of the earth."

"I have nothing for you to do there," said the old woman, "but you can give me your long black hair. You must know yourself that it is beautiful, and it pleases me. You can take my white hair for it, and that is always something."

"If you ask for nothing more," said she, "I will give you that gladly." And she gave her beautiful hair and received in exchange the old woman's white hair.

And then they went into the great hothouse of Death, where flowers and trees were growing marvellously together. There stood the fine hyacinths under glass bells, and there stood large, sturdy peonies; there grew water-plants, some quite fresh, others somewhat sickly; water-snakes were twining about them, and black crabs clung tightly to the stalks. There stood gallant palm trees, oaks, and plantains, and parsley and blooming thyme. Each tree and flower had its name; each was a human life: the people were still alive,

one in China, another in Greenland, scattered about in the world. There were great trees thrust into little pots, so that they stood quite crowded, and were nearly bursting the pots; there was also many a little weakly flower in rich earth, with moss round about it, cared for and tended. But the sorrowful mother bent down over all the smallest plants, and heard the human heart beating in each, and out of the millions she recognised that of her child.

"That is it!" she cried, and stretched out her hands over a little blue crocus flower, which hung down quite sick and pale.

"Do not touch the flower," said the old dame; "but place yourself here; and when Death comes—I expect him every minute—then don't let him pull up the plant, but threaten him that you will do the same to the other plants; then he'll be frightened. He has to account for them all; not one may be pulled up till he receives commission from Heaven."

And all at once there was an icy cold rush through the hall, and the blind mother felt that Death was arriving.

"How did you find your way hither?" said he. "How have you been able to come quicker than I?"

"I am a mother," she answered.

And Death stretched out his long hands towards the little delicate flower; but she kept her hands tight about it, and held it fast; and yet she was full of anxious care lest she should touch one of the leaves. Then Death breathed upon

*And Death went away with her child into
the unknown land.*

[See Page 268]

her hands, and she felt that his breath was colder than the icy wind; and her hands sank down powerless.

"You can do nothing against me," said Death.

"But the merciful God can," she replied.

"I only do what He commands," said Death. "I am His gardener. I take all His trees and flowers, and transplant them into the great Paradise gardens in the unknown land. But how they will flourish there, and how it is there, I may not tell you."

"Give me back my child," said the mother; and she implored and wept. All at once she grasped two pretty flowers with her two hands, and called to Death, "I'll tear off all your flowers, for I am in despair."

"Do not touch them," said Death. "You say you are so unhappy, and now you would make another mother just as unhappy!"

"Another mother?" said the poor woman; and she let the flowers go.

"There are your eyes for you," said Death. "I have fished them up out of the lake; they gleamed up quite brightly. I did not know that they were yours. Take them back—they are clearer now than before—and then look down into the deep well close by. I will tell you the names of the two flowers you wanted to pull up, and you will see their whole future, their whole human life; you will see what you were about to frustrate and destroy."

And she looked down into the well, and it was a happi-

ness to see how one of them became a blessing to the world, how much joy and gladness was diffused around her. And the woman looked at the life of the other, and it was made up of care and poverty, misery and woe.

"Both are the will of God," said Death.

"Which of them is the flower of misfortune, and which the blessed one?" she asked.

"That I may not tell you," answered Death; "but this much you shall hear, that one of these two flowers is that of your child. It was the fate of your child that you saw —the future of your own child."

Then the mother screamed aloud for terror.

"Which of them belongs to my child? Tell me that! Release the innocent child! Let my child free from all that misery! Rather carry it away! Carry it into God's kingdom! Forget my tears, forget my entreaties, and all that I have done!"

"I do not understand you," said Death. "Will you have your child back, or shall I carry it to that place that you know not?"

Then the mother wrung her hands, and fell on her knees, and prayed to the good God.

"Hear me not when I pray against Thy will, which is at all times the best. Hear me not! Hear me not!" And she let her head sink down on her bosom.

And Death went away with her child into the unknown land.

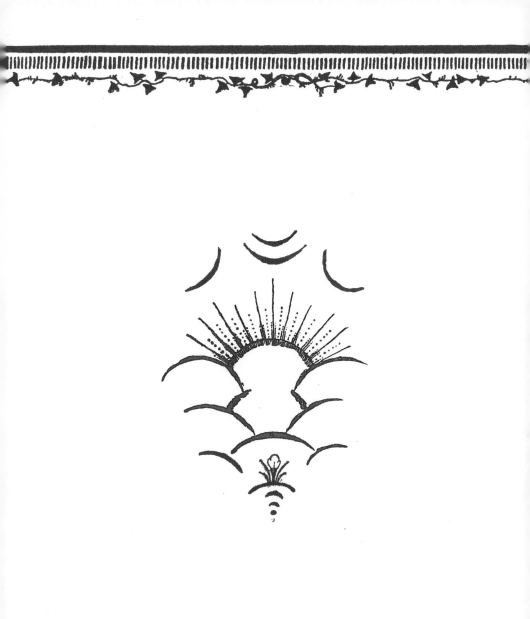